Herbert Barry

Ivan at Home

Or, pictures of Russian life

Herbert Barry

Ivan at Home
Or, pictures of Russian life

ISBN/EAN: 9783337295332

Printed in Europe, USA, Canada, Australia, Japan

Cover: Foto ©Andreas Hilbeck / pixelio.de

More available books at **www.hansebooks.com**

IVAN AT HOME;

OR,

PICTURES OF RUSSIAN LIFE.

By HERBERT BARRY,

AUTHOR OF "RUSSIA IN 1870," ETC. ETC.

WITH NUMEROUS ORIGINAL ILLUSTRATIONS.

LONDON:

THE PUBLISHING COMPANY, LIMITED,

7, QUALITY COURT, CHANCERY LANE, W.C.

1872.

SIRE,

WITH feelings of gratitude for your gracious reception of my work, "Russia in 1870," I venture to dedicate this new book to your Imperial Majesty,—the Liberator of the Russian people, and the Regenerator of the Russian Empire.

With the most profound respect, I am,

Sire,

Your Majesty's most obedient,

And humble Servant,

HERBERT BARRY.

LONDON, *April*, 1872.

PREFACE.

ENCOURAGED by the manner in which my last book on Russia was received, and seeing from that fact the interest that is felt at the present time in that Empire and her people, I have been led to essay these pictures of life and character.

In justice to myself, I must repeat that I do not pretend to any literary talent, but have endeavoured simply to recount the results of my own personal experience and observation.

I have taken the liberty of spelling the few Russian words that I have been obliged to use, in a manner that I thought a stranger ignorant of the language, going to the country, would the more easily understand.

It is necessary for me to say a word about the illustrations. I was anxious to have a few pictures in my book, in order the more fully to bring home some of the scenes to the reader; but the difficulty was to get true sketches. I therefore availed myself of the offer of some little girls, who proposed to attempt to sketch for me scenes so well known to them; and it is to their efforts that I am indebted for the majority of my pictures, whilst a few of them are from photographs taken for me by one of our village mujiks.

I have to thank Mr. Charles Eade for the manner in which he has carried out these simple though truthful designs.

Whilst this book was in the press, Mr. Ralston's new work* appeared; and if any of my readers should wish to know more about wedding and funeral customs, I refer them to that gentleman's

---

* "The Songs of the Russian People." By W. R. S. Ralston, M.A. London: Ellis & Green: 1872.

most exhaustive and lucid descriptions of the same.

Finally, I am very grateful to my critics, both here, in France, Germany, America, and Russia, for the leniency with which they treated "Russia in 1870," and trust they will find that I have in my present attempt taken advantage of many valuable suggestions they have given me.

April, 1872.

CONTENTS.

xii

Contents.

CHAPTER XX.

Contents.

LIST OF ILLUSTRATIONS.

IVAN AT HOME.

CHAPTER I.

A "BARRIN" AND HIS MODE OF LIVING.

IN a previous work I have mentioned that the names of Botacheff and Demidoff are now household words through the length and breadth of the Russian Empire.

These men, from blacksmiths, rose to be two of the richest proprietors in the kingdom, and by their own perseverance and intelligence became "Barrins" of those colossal metallurgical works which ever since have had no equal elsewhere. On their demise, their descendants were found to be another class—they had become aristocrats, and lived quite a different sort of life.

To repeat myself,—" The ' works ' as they are always called in Russia, are of a character peculiar to the country, and such as are not to be met with in other parts of the world ; in their enormous proportions, and their *modus operandi*, they are a peculiar Russian institution."

"Many of the establishments extend their operations over a space containing from three-quarters of a million to a million and a-half English acres : erect their works here and there where a favourable site exists, and thus form little principalities, containing numerous villages, which are entirely supported by the labour of the miners. It is easy to be seen that the proprietor of such an estate has immense influence over his dependent people, and that whereas great misery is caused when the works are badly managed, great comfort and happiness to the people result when they are well ordered."

" In the olden time, the ' Barrin ' lived in almost

princely style—in a palace surrounded by highly-ornamental gardens and extensive parks laid out with the most excellent taste. Such a man in the days of serfdom had all the state and authority of a monarch, enjoying unlimited and irresponsible power amongst his servile dependents."

Such, then, was a " Barrin."

The way he lived was so curious, and so different to the style of living found elsewhere in the world, that I believe it will be deemed interesting if I describe it.

" Barrin," really answering to " lord and master," is the word universally employed by the mujik when addressing his master ; but in all its fulness of meaning it can only be associated with such people as I am about to describe.

It was Ivan Ivanovitch C——, then, who found himself one day the inheritor of an estate exceeding a million and a-half of acres, together with forty-five villages and about sixty thousand inhabitants. On this estate were erected twenty-five large works for the production and manufacture of different metals. The revenue derived from this source yielded a princely income.

The principal palace on the property (for there were two,) was a fine stone building of magnificent proportions. On the grand story, or belle étage, Ivan Ivanovitch lived with his immediate family, occupying some twenty-four rooms, including a handsome reception hall.

Above, different members of the family, hangers on of all sorts, partook of the hospitality of their relation.

The ground-floor was devoted to kitchens, &c., and rooms containing the archives of the family, some of the papers amongst which dated as far back as the time of Peter the Great, when Ivan's ancestors were common workmen.

From the chief apartments led an orangerie, or, more properly speaking, a long winter-garden, in which Ivan Ivanovitch and his friends used to smoke their papirosses in the early spring-time, contemplating the beauties of the orange-trees and oleanders, which he had brought from Spain and Italy to decorate the barreness of his Russian home.

He had a billiard-table to amuse himself with on the long winter evenings, and his rooms were fitted up with pictures and *articles de luxe* from many towns in Europe. Not only the western hemisphere was searched for articles to adorn the house, but China and India both sent their stuffs and ornaments to decorate this Russian mansion. So what with China satin, Persian carpets, buhl furniture, and Italian pictures, Ivan Ivanovitch's house was something to look at.

To show the industry and natural intelligence of his mujiks, none but his own men had a hand in the building of the house. The fine parquet flooring, the cunningly-chased door-locks, the decorations on the wall, were all of them the peasant's invention and work—for the " Barrin " had not neglected the fine arts, and several of his men had been sent to the capital in order to learn the arts and mysteries of the finer branches of trade.

The living was on a scale equal to the other arrangements of the household. The cellar was full of the choicest wines; the farm on the estate yielded all the common necessaries of life, whilst Moscow being only five hundred miles away, there was not much difficulty in sending there for all the luxuries required.

The windows of the house looked out on to
gardens laid out and planted by a landscape
gardener, not with common pine and plane-trees,
but with shrubs and trees of every sort and
description. There were statues and fountains,
artificial water-courses, and all those little ornaments which go so far to assist Nature in
developing her beauties.

Properly trimmed walks led to forcing and
green-houses, where all manner of plants were
assembled, and where fruit of every variety existed
in abundance. It was all the same what your
fancy asked for here—pine-apples, strawberries,
peaches, grapes, plums, pears, cherries, or apples,
all were in quantities more than could be eaten.

Stables, calculated for a princely stud, were
always filled with the best horses which money
could buy, though, with the exception of occasional shooting excursions, Ivan Ivanovitch did
not himself often go out riding. He was too lazy
for such exercise.

At a comfortable distance from the house,
situated in the garden, and forming a pleasant
object in the landscape, was the theatre — a

building of by no means small pretensions, very handsomely decorated, and fitted up with dressing-rooms, &c., in a proper manner.

The "Barrin's" favourite amusement was attending the bi-weekly performances, and seeing French plays, translated into Russian, acted by his own mujiks; for the reader must bear in mind that all the actors and actresses were serfs, the principal portion of them having been specially educated for the purpose in Moscow.

The music was not bad—a stringed band for the theatre, and a full brass one for holiday occasions. This part of the establishment was always employed, and like everything else on the estate consisted of native talent.

Another amusement of the "Barrin's" was to have the whole of the grounds illuminated by means of variegated coloured lamps, on which his crest and coat of arms were most gorgeously displayed. When these were lighted, glittering among the branches in the gardens, the fountains murmuring in the distance, and the music playing some plaintive national song, the general *coup d'œil* was by no means ordinary.

At the end of the garden there was a considerable park, all the trees of which were planted like those in the other grounds. This park was full of deer, sheltered in the winter by proper houses, which, I am sorry to say, were much better than many of those in which the peasants lived.

The servants were very numerous, the principal ones dressed in liveries, bound with Ivan's crest and coat of arms, embroidered on yellow ribbon. They were, however, very lazy, and one man could only do one thing. For instance, a man was necessary to stand at the door, another to open it; one man employed his time in trimming the lamps and snuffing the candles; whereas the only duty of a fourth was to look after the Saints which were hung up in every room, and see that on the proper days the lights were burning before them. With the exception of a very few women to attend on the ladies of the house, the servants were all males. The kitchen-*maids* even were boys. The cook was a great man, never dirtying his own fingers with cooking, but only giving orders like an autocrat from his throne.

The dinners were superb; the service was good, and the appointments of the table all that could be desired. Ivan Ivanovitch had been to Paris and knew how things ought to be done.

It was a great day when the local Governor came to dine, for Ivan would be a little nervous as to whether certain of his late doings had been reported to his Excellency. On these occasions, everything and everybody would be on their best behaviour; the card-playing would be higher than usual, and before the great man took his departure on the following morning, a pretty good sum would have to be brought out of the strong room in the office, as the result of his winnings.

On other occasions in this house the card-playing was not extravagant, as the only man who had any sum to lose was the " Barrin; " his relations were played out: and Ivan, with all his extravagance, was much too wideawake to play against himself only.

The customs at these great dinners were curious; the host did not sit down, but ran about from guest to guest, to see that all were properly attended to. The host, however, proposed all the toasts, which were drunk with a full glass and emptied to the dregs. The dwarf of the house—for in these establishments he was a necessary addition—ran about the room during dinner, saying a word to this one and a word to another. Some servant, who had a particularly good ear for music, was in the room, and accompanied by his " bellalika " or guitar, sang national songs.

During dinner the drinking was furious,—principally champagne—but with the last course it finished; the ladies and gentlemen rose: if intimate, kissed the host and hostess on the cheek; if not, merely on the hand. Then followed smoking: not that it only just commenced, for you might have observed that His Excellency the Governor lighted a papiross immediately after his soup, and had been smoking at intervals during all the dinner time. Coffee and tea followed—the latter preferred—when all adjourned for a comfortable nap, a two hours' sleep being necessary to every Russian after dinner.

A Russian's grace before eating is simply crossing himself; the same manner of thanksgiving is gone through when the meal is finished.

Ivan Ivanovitch was a very quiet man when the Governor was with him, but a bit of a devil when he was away. The governor is the representative of the Czar in his government, and holds very great powers, particularly if he happens to be Military or General Governor; and Ivan Ivanovitch was not quite comfortable in his feelings regarding the man he had had put into the blast furnace a few days before, and rumours had been circulated concerning somebody or something he had blocked up in a wall in the cellar.

On one occasion a play was being performed in the theatre, the *denouement* of which did not suit Ivan Ivanovitch: the heroine, in his opinion, not having married the right person.

Ivan was furious, and immediately ordered the spectacle to be stopped, sent for the Pope, and insisted upon the hero and heroine being instantly married, and this order was actually carried out.

Church was a favourite place of resort for the " Barrin." There are no seats in a Russian church, as standing or kneeling down is the only form of worship known. A considerable portion of the

church was therefore railed off, in which the inhabitants of the Gospotsky Dom* could say their
prayers apart from the common herd. Ivan gave
away a good deal in charity, that being the only
salve to his conscience for the wrong he might
have done during the week. He also fasted
rigorously during the time named by the Church,
and, in consequence, usually ate himself into a fit
the first day he returned to his general way of
living.

The " Barrin " had more ways than one of obtaining the notice of the Czar. Ivan was a general,
and invited the whole regiment of cavalry which
he nominally commanded, to come and see him.
The Emperor gave the necessary permission, and
down they came, a nice crowd, some thousand
strong, with the usual complement of officers.
These our friend feasted and fêted for a month,
receiving as the reward of his patriotism and for
his outlay, a star of some coveted order.

I fancy this was the crowning-point of the
" Barrin's " happiness, as in one of his portraits I

---

* Gentleman's house.

noticed the famous camp displayed in the distance, whilst Ivan Ivanovitch himself is arrayed in all the magnificence of his military costume.

He had curious ideas on many points. On one occasion a hurricane was threatening the safety of one of the dams of his numerous lakes. He got frightened, but had heard that a line of men were, from their elasticity, a good thing to support a heavy pressure; he therefore called out two thousand of his workmen, whom he placed in double line on the lee-side of this bank or dam. The elements, however, asserted their sway, and the dam gave way, carrying many of the mujiks with it.

In spite of all this, the men had much to thank their master for. Not far from the palace, on the side of a charming lake, he erected a pavilion, and surrounded it with pretty gardens, and here, on great holidays, he used to entertain his people with music and amusements, accompanied always with abundant supplies of refreshment.

The master also kept a good eye over his hospital, an establishment which, according to law, he was obliged to keep up from his own funds. It was a fine building, with 150 beds in it, well supplied with everything required, having a dispensary, in which the drugs were prepared and dispensed on a liberal scale. When a Russian peasant is dosed, he wants a good bowl-full of medicine, and something that tastes strong and nasty.

There were several officials of the Government living upon the estate; perhaps the less said about them the better; they always hung on to Ivan Ivanovitch's skirts, and took their meals at the bottom of his table.

Great days in the house were those holy days upon which the Popes came to bless anew the pictorial images. The whole household would be present whilst the ceremony was being performed, at the close of which, the chief Pope would hold the cross to be kissed by the faithful. The "Barrin" approached first and kissed the relic, and afterwards the Pope's hand. The household followed in their order of seniority. The Pope then shut up the cross, together with his cap, in a box like a fiddle-case, and all sat down to lunch or dinner.

The amount of liquor those Popes drank was enormous, and they mostly became intoxicated.

On one occasion, on a celebration of this sort, I had proposed the health of the Emperor, when a Pope jumped up, ran to the saint in the corner, and began praying for the Czar ; before he had half-finished the prayer he tumbled down dead-drunk under the image. The other Popes present merely laughed at the circumstance, but did not think any the worse of their brother for this little episode.

A favourite amusement of Ivan Ivanovitch used to be to sit in a great gilt throne at one end of the hall, whilst the peasants danced French quadrilles to the strains of the music from the other end of the room ; and woe betide any unfortunate wight who made a false step ; he would be pretty sure to get the rod in the morning.

Every attribute which could add to the comfort of a household was to be found under that roof : butcher, pastry-cook, tailor, shoemaker, hair-dresser,—all were at the disposal of the dwellers in the house. The poor hair-dresser has, unfortunately, outlived his time. He is now an assistant in the blast furnace, and, I am told, is never to be depended upon to follow his profession after 9 a.m., owing to his love of vodka. I was rash enough to ignore this information, and ordered him up to operate on me after his guaranteed time; the consequence was he nearly cut my ear off as well as my hair.

Ivan kept up all great State holidays, such as the Emperor's birthday, &c., with great rejoicings. "Barrins" were very loyal subjects as long as their men were serfs.

In addition to the two palaces in the country, which Ivan Ivanovitch owned, he had also one of the finest of the Moscow houses. This, a perfect palace, was furnished even more luxuriously than his country homes. In fact, no finer lodgings could be found in Moscow for our Ambassador, when sent to assist at the coronation of the present Czar, than this very house.

There Ivan Ivanovitch had his own private church, and held a complete court on a small scale. When he travelled from the country to the town, he did so in comparative state. No lumbering tarantass did he trust his limbs in, but in a handsome travelling-carriage, drawn by eight horses, did he while away the time on the road. Ivan knew what was needed to make his journey comfortable, and this carriage was fitted up most luxuriously. The seats and sides were shifting, and contained every necessary, eatable and drinkable. The accommodation on the road was uncomfortable in those days, and the "Barrin" never got out of his carriage until he arrived in Moscow.

Concerts, very respectable even for Moscow, were given by the "Barrin's" own people; but town life did not suit him as well as country life, and it was not often the Muscovite capital saw his face. In the great city Ivan was surrounded by many more of his own class and standing, and was not regarded as a king; this was not to his taste, or, for that matter, to that of any of the other mighty masters, and so these "Barrins" generally remained in their country homes.

The "Barrin" had travelled abroad—he had been to France, had a villa at Florence, a château in Spain, and had thus acquired many of his extravagant ideas from foreign countries. To his great annoyance, his own women could not,

or would not, wash his Paris-made shirts as well
as they were done in the French capital. Never
mind; that grievance need not bother him—there
was a way out of it. He could send his shirts
to Paris to be washed, and he actually did so.

But his house and establishment had one want
—Eastern he was in all his ideas and manners,
and a harem he must have. None of his native
workmen knew the style of building required.
That was of no consequence. Could he not send
to Constantinople for plans and patterns? He
did this; and in course of time the harem was
built and finished after a perfect Eastern model.
There were the divans, the coloured-glass windows, reflecting their rosy hue on the marble
statuary. The china seats and the little carpets
all showed their Eastern origin, and, in fact, all
was Turkish.

But the harem must be tenanted: this did not
trouble Ivan much. Was he not lord and master
of upwards of twenty thousand slaves? True,
these were uneducated, but that was to be
remedied; and so many of the youngest women
were sent to Moscow, for a few months, to

be a little polished, and soon the 'harem was full.

By this time Ivan's style of life had begun to tell upon him: he was getting an old man, too; and there were growing signs among the serfs which showed that their stolid patience was giving way under the iniquities beneath which they daily groaned.

The Government sent more inspectors to see what was going on, and in spite of Ivan's orders to the contrary, these officials found their way to the Gospotsky Dom. There was a deep and wide river, which every one coming to call upon him had to pass. Ivan found this very handy when a more scrupulous officer than usual was sent to report the "Barrin's" doings. If the unwelcome official succeeded in getting *on* the river, he very rarely got *across* it; and nothing more was heard or known of him.

The "Barrin's" income was also getting small, and no wonder, when the reader has heard what he did with his money. Once he looked after his affairs personally, but by-and-by he bethought him of getting foreigners about him.

He engaged Germans, who he had heard in his travels were sober, thrifty, careful people. So they were; but whilst his Russians robbed him only, these Germans literally skinned him. This was not the worst, they skinned his mujiks, too; and the poor devils naturally thought it was done by the order of the master.

Now came the dark side of the picture: the peasants would neither work nor pay; the ready money was exhausted; the works produced nothing; the German *employés* stole everything that was to be found: the estate was pawned to the Government: Ivan Ivanovitch was ruined. He was a fool, or else he could have surmounted his difficulties; but he did not try. He had still other small estates in different parts of the empire, upon which, anyhow, he could subsist. Like the peasants, he shrugged his shoulders with a sigh, and with "It is the act of God," went to sleep.

He began to borrow money at most usurious rates of interest—that is to say, not exactly of interest, for a usury law existed which was only repealed a few months ago, but the commission,

&c., charged amounted to the same thing. This kept him going a little while.

Then came the worst feature. The mujiks began to burn the forests, the works, the heaps of charcoal; the workmen smashed the machinery; a small insurrection commenced. The theatre was half-pulled down; the windows of the orangerie and glass-houses were broken; the horses were turned loose from the stables; the very furniture was stolen from the house; and, as a crowning act, the principal palace was attempted to be fired.

Ivan Ivanovitch died: the change was too great for him to bear. He was buried with the pomp and ceremony of an emperor; cannons announced his entry into his grave; the trappings of his coffin were magnificent; the treat to the peasantry was princely; every robe every priest wore was new for the occasion; and no funeral had ever surpassed this one in extravagance.

Of course, money was wanted for all this. The rich peasants supplied it. Their Ivan Ivanovitch and "Barrin," although, as they expressed it, "having gone to the devil," must still be buried in a manner suitable to his greatness; and funds were freely supplied to accomplish this most necessary end.

Ivan Ivanovitch had been forced to make many changes during the last few months of his life.

The theatre was closed; the harem was tenantless; the cellar was empty; in short, the glories of the place had departed.

It was about time, for on the next day to that which saw the earth cover up Ivan Ivanovitch, the Crown took possession of his estate.

He left two sons,—of course, totally ruined.

It is not my wish, nor would it interest my readers, to recount the rapid manner in which, under the Government tutor, the poor " Barrin's " estate now went down lower and lower into the depths of ruin. This individual cheated in every possible way he could.

" Everybody robbed in every conceivable way; every dodge was adopted to cloak the system and manner of robbing; the proprietors were denuded of everything; the wood cut down on the properties, not a stick being left; the very works themselves robbed of their machinery; every piece of metal that could be turned into money taken out; the works allowed to tumble down; not an atom of repair done to the buildings; while the tutor was making an immense fortune out of the estate."

In the result, the unfortunate sons got nothing.

My readers will hardly believe me, when, knowing they are living in this year anno domini eighteen hundred and seventy-two, I tell them that the family sketch I have written could have been seen any time previously and down to the year eighteen hundred and sixty-one, and that, leaving out the incidents in the life, which are impossible now that the mujiks are free men, and the new law is in force, the same examples of living exist in a few solitary instances even now in the remoter parts of Russia.

The story I have recounted is a perfectly true one, even in the minutest details; some of the incidents occurred before my time. These were all given to me on the most trustworthy information by a living witness. Almost all the actors are now "dead; several of them I have assisted to lay in their graves; and what descendants do exist of this ancient family, who were in affluence for one hundred and eighty years, have not now one single copeck.

Their estates are in the hands of foreigners; their houses are desecrated by the presence of strangers; their peasants are free men. Order and regularity have again succeeded to riot and rapine; and the same state of prosperity and plenty exists as it did in the time of the Great Peter.

I have endeavoured in this sketch to give, not only an account of the manners and customs of these Russian "Barrins," but also by showing their manner of living, their riotous and improper life, their total disregard of everything that was really good, their utter disregard of to-morrow— to account for their rapid fall; and I believe that all must agree with me in thinking that it is a happy thing for the country and people of Russia that one of the names fast disappearing from their country is that of " Barrin."

CHAPTER II.

THE VILLAGE DOCTOR.

IT was an unfortunate day for me when my predecessor in office appointed Doctor X—— to look after the health of the people on our estates.

The Doctor's most important business was superintending the hospital, in which there were generally some thirty or forty patients; after which, the whole of the villages had to be attended to, and for this purpose he had four assistants or under-surgeons.

An apothecary dispensed the medicines that the Doctor ordered,—an arrangement, I think, decidedly beneficial for the patients.

Where X—— obtained his degree I could never understand, but by some means he was enabled to write M.D. after his name. He had been engaged, before he honoured us with his presence, in travelling about in the suite of some old noble-woman. This is the general employment of young Russian doctors, as every well-regulated household must have its doctor or medical man.

Even in these remote villages, the professional etiquette is the same as in the cities. All pre-scriptions must be written on proper forms, and entered regularly in books kept for the purpose; moreover, every dispenser of medicine must be duly licensed.

Peter the Great, amongst many more of his practical ordinances, issued a ukase that none but Germans might practise as apothecaries, as he said that his own Russians were such dolts, they would be continually poisoning his subjects by mistake, whilst he could depend upon the Germans. Our apothecary was consequently half a German, and that fact, in the peasants' ideas, made the medicines he dispensed more disagreeable to swallow.

The assistant-surgeons were not very well acquainted with the mysteries of their profession, and their duties were principally confined to tooth-drawing and vodka-drinking; any bad case of accident or illness had to depend upon the skill of the Doctor for a cure.

Now, Gospodin X——, if not a great *phy*sician, was a great *mu*sician, and, I am afraid, paid more attention to, and took more interest in, crotchets and quavers than he did in his patients. The people were continually complaining to me that he treated them much more in a musical than he did in a doctorly manner.

That they were right in their complaints the following story will show :—

A peasant came to the house, and begged to see me. I learnt that he was a poor fellow who had just broken his arm, and told the servants to let him in.

" Well, Ivan, what is the matter ? How is your arm ? " I asked.

" Very bad, Barrin ! " be replied.

" Why don't you go to the Doctor ? " I added.

" It does not seem to be much good to do so,"

replied the mujik. " I went to him just now, and this is all I got by it! I rang the bell, and asked to see the Doctor. Presently he came to the door with his violin in his hand, and noticing my arm was bandaged up, said, playing a tune on his fiddle meanwhile, ' Well, what's the matter with your arm ? ' ' It's broken, Vassily Vassilyvitch ! ' With another tune on the fiddle, he added, ' Show it to me ; ' to which I replied, ' Oh ! I didn't come here to see a fool, but a doctor ! ' and so came away to tell you how he treated me."

DROWNED, BECAUSE HE HAD NO CROSS.

CHAPTER III.

SUPERSTITIONS.

THE superstitious regard which the peasants have for the types and emblems of their religion, cannot be better illustrated than by recounting the following :—

I was looking out of the open window one beautiful evening in summer, listening to the echoes as they came wafted across the lake at my feet, not knowing which to admire most,—the simplicity of the chant, or the occupation of the singing boys in the boat, as they sat so contentedly tending their fishing-lines.

It is such sights as these that cause the looker-on almost to envy the now quiet and contented life of the mujik.

It was Sunday; a number of people were passing along the road, returning from church. Presently a man—evidently reeling. drunk, but not absolutely stupefied—turned off the road, and deliberately walked into the lake.

The people on the bank stood and looked at him, but not one of them tried to arrest his progress or frustrate his intentions. Into the water the man walked, further and further, until getting. to a spot where it was deeper, he disappeared suddenly.

I could hardly believe my senses, but imagined the man had some friends on the shore looking after him; but, to my astonishment, no one moved, or took any trouble to help him. I rushed out, and ran to the lake, had drags fetched, and in time dragged up the body,—of course, quite dead.

In due time the police arrived, and made their

inquest, and the body was handed over to the relatives. Then came the great question : How was it the man was drowned ?

It is the universal custom in Russia, amongst the members of the orthodox Church, whether they be princes or peasants, to suspend to their children's necks when infants, a small cross, generally attached by a metal chain to ensure its safety; should this cross be lost by any means, another must immediately replace it.

Now, in the present case, the clothes of the poor man were carefully examined, then the body, and, on looking to his neck, no cross was to be seen. This immediately settled the question, and the verdict amongst the villagers was this : " Drowned because he had no cross on his neck !"

On another occasion, passing through a small town on the banks of the Oka, in the Government of Tambov, I called upon the merchant to whom I had let the right of fishing in a considerable extent of the river, in order to buy some sterlet. This is the most famous fish in the empire, and really a great delicacy. We have no fish in England at all equal to it in richness and flavour;

and thus Russians, passing a sterlet fishery, always endeavour to secure a fish dinner.

I went with the proprietor to see his fish-tanks, and select my fish. We saw several, but the man was continually poking about with his net, endeavouring to stir into activity a very large fish which he said was there.

The water was much discoloured, and we had a difficulty in catching even a passing glimpse of the dainty. We succeeded, however, in doing so at last, and then came the question of price.

"Now," said the merchant, "the price of that fish was ten roubles, but yesterday the head Pope, having heard of it, paid me a visit of inspection, and was so pleased with the sight of it, that he blessed it; and so I should not like to take less than fifteen roubles for it to-day."

I thought the man was joking with me, but I found he was quite serious, and would not abate one copeck of his price.

Whether the Pope had a commission in the five roubles I cannot say.

Of the "childlike duty and respect" with which we have been told by a recent writer on

" Free Russia " the parish priest is treated by his parishioners, I have seen too many examples to the contrary to be able to deceive myself on the subject.

I remember making the acquaintance of one priest, at a village which had caught fire in the night, about a dozen versts from our works. As usual, I was summoned to the scene, and when I arrived, found the invariable sight on such occasions—nearly half the village in flames at once, and from those houses not yet burning, the owners were very leisurely removing their goods and chattels in the following order :—

First, the pictures of saints were reverently taken down from their corner cupboards; after which, the mujik took his box, containing his little " all; " placing this in the middle of the street, he returned, and removing the small windows from their frames, laid them carefully on the chest. To these he added his few other worldly possessions, such as pots and pans, &c., and then quietly going out into the street, he sat on his goods, and waited until the flames attacked his house, hardly ever attempting to stay the progress of the conflagration, and in answer to any inquiries as to the reason he was not exerting himself, replied, "It is the will of God."

On the walls, or gate-post of every house in all villages in Russia a small board is hung, bearing a picture of the particular implement the owner is bound to produce and use at any fire that may occur. These are such things as water-buckets, ladders, long poles, &c.; but they are seldom to be seen when the catastrophe really happens, and such is the blind belief or the fatalism of the Russian peasant, that I found it quite impossible in these village fires to make the natives pull down a house or two to prevent the spread of the conflagration, but invariably had to bring men from a distant village for the purpose.

As I observed then, this fire did not differ from other village fires. My brigade had arrived with their engines, and the women were busily drawing water from their wells to supply them. The individual superintending this work was the Pope. Unfortunately it was Sunday night, and he was very drunk, staggering about with difficulty.

As he reeled up to salute me he fell, and at the same moment the counterpoise at the end of the beam, which is always used in that part of Russia to draw water with, came heavily down on the back of his head.

I ran to pick him up. " Never mind him," said the woman who was at the well, " The *pig*, he is used to it."

Again, sometimes the priests return the compliment.

I used to make it a rule to contribute pretty largely to the wants of the church and clergy, as I felt that the accident of the property having fallen into the hands of foreigners ought not to militate against the receipts of the Popes, and they made this a great argument in their appeals to their parishioners.

I once heard one of them abusing his people on the subject in church. Are you not ashamed of yourselves, you who call yourselves Russians and good? You give nothing to the Church; you are a miserable lot, you let foreigners come here, and it is they who support the Church; while you, who ought to give, do nothing. " Oh !" he concluded, as if he were winding up everything in one word, " you are pigs ! "

. The Popes themselves are not very particular as to the way in which they celebrate their church ceremonies, although I am bound to say they never allow the services to be neglected.

A new church was to be consecrated, and it was necessary that I should be present during a particular part of the ceremony. I did not wish to go at the commencement and wait throughout, so arranged with the head Pope that he should send me word by a Cossack when I was wanted, who was ordered to wait for the purpose.

On arriving at the proper time I went in to the inner altar, where all the Popes were assembled, the chief of them reading with his face turned towards the people who literally crammed the church.

Immediately the old man saw me, he interrupted his reading to shake hands with and ask me how I was; then remarking he feared I should find myself very cold, returned to his reading or praying whichever it was.

He finished, when another Pope took his place,

and was commencing to read a prayer, when he was immediately pulled away by another Pope, who claimed the turn. A regular row began as to who was to be the successful party; meanwhile one of the deacons, probably afraid of the scandal this scene would cause among the people, came to the front, and chanted in his immensely deep bass voice, " Gospodi pomeelui !" (God have mercy upon us !), during which time the popes had settled the matter of precedence amicably, and the service proceeded.

CHAPTER IV.

WEDDINGS AND WEDDING CUSTOMS.

THE Greek Church does not allow the sacrament of marriage to be partaken of on any of the great fasts : the days for weddings in Russia are therefore few.

Amongst the mujiks, marriages for love are rare. The question asked of the " Proposeress," who arranges the village matrimonial affairs, was in the olden time, " Is Sascha a good hard worker ? " whilst now it is, " What can Sascha pay ? "

A common mujik's wedding, with its accompaniments of drinking at the Traktir, and the bacchanalian dance in which the immediate friends, disguised in grotesque costumes, join in the public streets, is decidedly a demoralizing affair; but the wedding customs of the respectable middle class have many points of interest.

Young Michael was enamoured of Maria Andraevna, but her parents would not hear of the match, for the " Proposeress " had told them, what the old man already knew, that Michael had no means, while he himself was warm with roubles, and had but this one daughter.

Maria, however, wished to marry Michael, and turned a deaf ear to all the arguments of the father in favour of the man he had picked out from many eligible suitors as the one most to his taste.

Maria really liked Michael, and refused to be comforted: so after a while, as the bloom faded from her cheek and the wrinkles began to appear, old Andrew relented, and gave his consent; for under any circumstances he could reap some benefit from the marriage, for the lad was managing clerk to his opponent in business, and by taking him into his own service he would learn the tricks of his neighbour's dealings.

The position of the bride's father was that of a very small tradesman, but, as I have before said, he had plenty of roubles.

Now the great question of dowry had to be discussed; for although some articles, such as the wedding suit of clothes, a dressing-gown, and many shirts, were in every case necessary presents from the bride to her groom, other things had to be arranged for privately.

The Russians are exceedingly strict in the manner in which these agreements for dowry are fulfilled. Memory is too shifting to trust with such weighty details, and so paper contracts are written, every stipulated article of which engagement must be carried out *before* the ceremony is performed.

These difficulties were at length settled to the satisfaction of all parties, and the day for the wedding arrived.

The bridegroom's house displayed the results of his skilful management, and there, arranged in one room were the presents paid for by the bride's father. A handsome feather-bed, with embroidered sheets, and a magnificent crimson satin coverlet, six eider-down pillows to match, a Persian carpet by the bedside, two or three silk dresses, and the bridegroom's smart dressing-gown were suspended on a stand in the corner of the room.

In another chamber, numerous linen under-garments were displayed, including fourteen dozen shirts, which were considered as sufficient to last Michael for the rest of his life. A rich black velvet " shouba " for Maria, together with a similar winter garment in cloth for the husband, were also exhibited hanging on the wall.

Numerous boots and shoes, bonnets and table linen completed the list according to contract, which included the suit of black cloth which Michael wore at that moment.

The bride was then inspected in her father's home. Sitting in all the splendour of white silk, veil, and orange blossoms, she appeared faint, and anxious for the service to commence; and no wonder, for her Church allowed nothing to pass her lips from the previous sunset until after the solemnization of the marriage.

The ceremony in the church was pretty.

The bride and bridegroom held a lighted taper in their hands, in front of a small altar placed in the centre of the church. Rings were placed on their fingers, and their hands being joined, they were led by the Pope three times round the altar. Two highly-ornamented gilt crowns were placed on their heads and held over them by the groomsmen during part of the service. They drank wine out of a cup three times, and kissing one another, the ceremony was finished.

The married couple then made the tour of the church, crossing themselves at and saluting each saintly Icon on their way.

Weddings generally take place towards evening, so that immediately after the ceremony dinner commences at the house of the bride's father.

At a marriage feast lighted candles are placed in every position and corner possible. No other wine but champagne should be drunk, and the quantity consumed of this beverage is remarkable.

The dinner is followed by a ball, and the feasting is usually kept up for twenty-four hours.

The custom of honey-mooning does not exist

A WEDDING DANCE.

To face p. 42.

in Russia. The married couple spend the first few days of their wedded life with the bride's father.

Shortly after the marriage the bride and bridegroom must call upon every one of their relations, friends, and acquaintances, and after this ceremony is finished they sink back into their ordinary life.

CHAPTER V.

FUNERALS AND FUNERAL CUSTOMS.

A RUSSIAN funeral is not a pleasant sight; many of the customs, both in and out of the Church, have still a remnant of barbarism about them, which it is to be hoped may be soon changed.

In fact, "death" in Russia is so hedged in with formalities of every sort, both religious and civil, that, for some considerable time after the spirit has passed away, it can be truly said, "there is no peace for the dead."

Supposing, for example, a person suddenly dies or is killed; according to Russian law, the body must remain untouched by any one, on that very same spot, until the police have arrived, and made their report. This regulation, however useful for the elucidation of the inquiry, is very disagreeable to the neighbours. I have known a body to be left in a public thoroughfare for a fortnight, in the middle of summer.

The mujiks are so afraid of being implicated in any case of murder or accident, that if a body is discovered by them half dead, as a rule they will not give any immediate help or relief, but first run off to find the representative of the law.

I remember, on one occasion, whilst travelling in the Government of Vladimir, seeing a man lying by the road-side with his throat cut from ear to ear. I was anxious to get out of the tarantass to see whether he was dead. The post-boy would not listen to me, and drove his horses all the faster, whilst explaining that it would be the most dangerous thing for me to do to go near the body, as, by so doing, I should get mixed up in the affair, and very likely the police would accuse me of the crime itself. So nervous was the man, that upon his arrival in his village he did not even report the case to the Starosta.

On several occasions I have been called to accidents in the mines, which, by-the-bye, are not "mines" according to our ideas, but simply small wells dug out of the sand, and in which the miners are very fond of grubbing without taking the precaution to support the sides with the staves supplied to them for the purpose. The sides of these holes are, in consequence, often falling in, and the men at the bottom of them stand a chance of being suffocated, if not immediately released. In these cases, it is even difficult to get the men to dig among the sand to extricate their comrade, so fearful are they of being accused by the police of complicity in the accident.

In ordinary cases of death, three days and two nights are allowed to elapse before burial, during which time, hired mourners are invariably employed to watch the body. These mourners are supposed to pray the whole time of their watch, and a deacon or sacristan ought also to be present chanting different portions of the Burial Service.

The procession from the house to the church is headed by the nearest relation of the departed, who carries the saintly picture belonging to his friend, holding it up in both hands in front of him. According to the wealth of the person being buried, more or fewer Popes accompany the procession, chanting by the way, and with their banners and saints, making rather an imposing show. Incense is also burned on the route, for the apparent reason of sanctifying the dead body.

The churches on these occasions will always be full, a Russian never omitting an opportunity of seeing a show of any sort in his church—whether it be a funeral or a marriage is all the same to him.

Every person present at the church should carry a lighted taper, which tapers are supplied to the public at the expense of the friends of the deceased.

The coffin is laid on trestles in the middle of the church; the lid is not fixed on, but stands by the side, and the face of the dead is consequently exposed to view.

The coffin of a man of rank is very showily decorated, covered with velvet, and much trumpery embroidery; whilst the poor man is laid in his last resting-place in the commonest of deal boxes.

After the ceremony, which appears to be all finished in the church, the friends of the deceased file round the coffin, and imprint a kiss on the forehead of the corpse. This practice is very disagreeable, and obviously unhealthy; in the summer-time, the smell is hardly counteracted by the abundant use of incense about the building.

The coffin is then nailed down, and carried below to the vault, where it is placed in a common tin covering.

A service for the dead should be held in the church daily for forty days after the funeral; and inasmuch as the spirit is supposed to inhabit the house which the body has just left, several services ought to be held there during the same term.

At the funerals of common people, boiled rice is taken by the relatives to the cemetery, and there eaten, I have been told.

The attention which the better classes of the Russians pay to their lost relatives is something charming to behold.

In our principal village lived an old Count, the last of a long race of mighty aristocrats. The remains of his wife and only son and daughter rested in the vaults of the church. On every single day of his life that that old man was at home, did he visit this vault and pray there; and when going on, or returning from, a journey, his last and first acts were to pray for the rest of the souls of his lost family. Many and many a time has this poor old man told me he was going to pray over *all* he had now left him in this world, and I thought of the truth of his remark when I followed this descendant of a powerful race to his grave, and helped to lay him in the vault, which was the only remnant left him of a princely fortune, none but strangers and foreigners being there to pay this last respect to his ancient name.

To return to my subject. The funeral being

over, the party adjourn to the family mansion, upon entering which many peculiarities will be observed :— the serving-men are all dressed in black clothes, bound with white ribbon; the looking-glasses are all taken from the walls; the pictures are unhung and packed away out of sight; in many instances, the curtains will be withdrawn from the windows; in fact, all looks desolate, with the exception of the dining-tables, which are placed in several rooms, and, covered as they are with choice wines, augur well for the feast that will probably follow.

The first thing that takes place on the arrival of the Popes, is the manufacture and brewing of a drink principally composed of honey. The Popes help with this, and, after apparently blessing it, say some prayer before the pictured saint, which is suspended in the corner of every room in a Russian house. The drink is then passed round, in the manner of a loving cup, all the company take a sip, and, as far as I could understand, drink to the rest of the friend just buried.

In a short time after this dinner is served, and, from my experience, these dinners are generally very noisy ones. The Popes and deacons take a part in them, and vie with the laymen in the noise they make. The nearest relative takes the chief place at the table, and, from some examples I saw, does not seem to be much affected by the ceremony just performed. He appears to challenge his guests continually to drink, and generally to enjoy himself.

After dinner, smoking, tea, and card-playing *ad libitum*, for those who like it, are the order of the day.

I was myself so much astonished at what I saw at one of these entertainments after a Russian funeral, that, knowing the family to be most respectable and very religious, and withal that the gentleman entertaining us dearly loved his young wife, whom we had just laid in her grave, I inquired from one well able to tell me, what it all meant.

His answer was this: " This feasting, eating, and drinking, is carried on only because it is supposed that by these means the sorrow of our friend will be assuaged, and that for the time at least his grief will be drowned. There are people

here amongst us who seldom drink anything but
water, but to-day they will drink champagne
until they burst, in order to show their apprecia-
tion of their friend and thus help him to drown
his sorrow.''

CHAPTER VI.

VILLAGE POPES.

FATHER NATHANIEL was the head Pope or priest on our property. He was distinguished from his many brethren by being a gentleman, from having received a liberal education (he could read Latin and Greek), but principally from his having in his younger days spent his leisure hours in giving instruction to the youth of his village.

Almost all the young people in the village who possessed any education were indebted for their

advantages to Father Nathaniel. This alone made
the man my friend, but even he was not free
from the clerical vice of drinking, and owed his
death to the inordinate consumption of vodka.

He died suffering greatly. The vodka got into
his limbs, and beginning with his feet mounted
up until the body became so saturated with the
spirit, that it was as if on fire. His only relief
was sitting in cold water, the depth being increased as the spirit mounted; at last it reached
his heart, and the Father died in his bath.

Father Peter was of a different sort: he was a
jolly, rollicking, ignorant, stupid fellow, fond of
a game of cards, but, having an out-of-the way
cure of souls, he had not many opportunities of
enjoying his favourite amusement.

But when the "Stanavoi" came on his rounds,
or the local Tchinovnik was in the village, then
high jinks were going on in the Pope's house.

One Saturday morning such a party commenced
their game of "preference," and went merrily on
until the bell began to summon the villagers to
their vespers. But the Father was deaf, and did
not hear the summons.

" Father Peter, Father Peter! come to church; the people are all waiting for you to begin the service," exclaimed the sacristan, rushing into the room.

" All right, Ivan, I'm coming," answered the Pope, and laying down his cards with a request to his friends to stay the game until he returned, he went to church and performed the service, at the close of which he went back, helped himself to a glass of vodka, and with an exclamation, " That *has* made me dry !" swallowed the spirit, sat down again to his cards and distraction.

The party played all night, for the Tchinovnik had done a good stroke of business in the neighbourhood, and was in funds: so that the Pope had not such a fine chance every day.

The hour for the Sunday morning service arrived, and the sacristan had again to call his superior, who reluctantly obeyed the call. Two hours after this the play recommenced, and continued until the early dawn on Monday morning. The Pope must have his amusements, but nothing was allowed to interfere with the punctual performance of the services.

Father Peter had very odd notions of the words " meum " and " tuum." I once gave him an order to receive some wood out of our forests. This order served him on several occasions, until, discovering the trick, I made him return it. Wood, however, he must have, so he helped himself, carrying on a regular business in stealing first, and then selling what did not belong to him.

I do not believe a Pope ought to smoke, and I never saw one doing so in public ; but in the small social gatherings we were accustomed to have, the reserve would wear off, and a good Havannah cigar tempt the Fathers. It was an odd sight, and did not add to their otherwise clerical appearance, as sitting round the table, amidst the quaffing of champagne, these men, with their long uncut hair, beards, and moustache (the orthodox Church does not permit her Popes to cut their hair), dressed in long loose robes, with cross suspended from the neck, were quietly smoking their cigars with all the enjoyment possible.

CHAPTER VII.

THE VILLAGE STARSHINA.

THE election for starshina or mayor had termi-
nated in Alexie Romanovitch Sheremetikoff
being exalted to that high office, an event which
the poor man deeply deplored, as he was a shopkeeper, and in consequence of his election must
now give up the supervision of his business, and
give the whole of his time to his civic duties.
Moreover, three years was the term for which he
must serve, and he would receive during that time
the magnificent salary of eight hundred roubles
(about one hundred pounds) a year, out of which
he has to pay the salaries of three clerks and
provide stationery for the office.

Alexie Romanovitch came to report his election to me immediately after the event, and, adorned with his chain and badge of office, looked well worthy of the dignity just conferred on him.

He commenced with, " Ah, Barrin, this is an unfortunate day in my life. Whoever would have thought they would have played me such a trick as electing me mayor?" and added, " I know what the pigs have done it for: they see I have the only flour-store here, and that I have nobody else to attend to my business but myself, and think that now I am mayor they will cheat my wife when they deal with her;" and then soliloquised, "but I'll be even with them: won't I make them pay up their taxes?"

And so Alexie was obliged to serve, as, if elected by the commune, there are no means of escaping from the office.

The starshina's position is not a comfortable one. In his town-hall, or "volost" as it is called, he is the executor of the commands received from the Ispravnik, or local chief of police. He must also carry out the orders received from the local arbitrators of peace. For these purposes he has "sotskys," or policemen, under him; these men are the village mujiks, drawn by lot, and their uniform consists of a brass badge and a walking-stick.

The starshina is likewise the president of tho communal republic, and, as chairman of the common council meetings, has to carry out their decisions.

This common council, elected by universal suffrage, has criminal and civil jurisdiction, whilst the starshina, in virtue of his office, also exercises notarial powers.

The mayor must also collect the town taxes, see that the starosta or head man of the village collects the lord's obrok or land-tax, and must levy on the goods and chattels of the peasants if this is not paid.

It can be easily understood from the above enumeration of his duties, that the position of mayor is not coveted by the Russians.

The man gets into hot water with everybody. The Ispravnik bullies him for not having collected the crown taxes; the arbitrator of peace complains of him to the governor; the common

council swear he does not carry out their deci-
sion; the peasants declare he makes them pay
double taxes; the Barrin says he cannot get
him to levy for his obrok; the starosta says he
bullies his peasants; and the local coroner or
judge declares that the commune was never in
such a bad state before.

As a result, the poor devil, whoever he may be,
retires from his office at the end of . his term with
the bad will of all, and generally minus what
little money he had scraped together before he
received his local rank.

Supposing such an event as a sudden death
by accident takes place, which the villagers may
have reason to suppose has been associated with
foul play, the · common council will hold an
inquest after the police have made their examination.

The council examine witnesses, and have power
to "send for persons and papers."

Some of these examinations of witnesses are
very curious.

A man had been drowned at one of the works.
It was winter time, and he had wandered from

the traktir on to the lake, across which he staggered on the ice until he arrived before the unfrozen waters at the sluice, into which he walked, and was only taken out the following day, in consequence of a report which the watchman on this sluice had made to the office, that a man had been drowned there.

Necessarily this watchman was examined as a chief witness, and the mayor asked him whether he had not heard anybody crying out, he replied,—

" Oh, yes ; I heard the cries, went to the sluice, and asked who and what it was making such a noise. The man then called out again, and said he should be drowned. I hollowed to him, and told him I could not see him. He repeated his cry, when I replied, what *is* the use of your crying out, if I cannot see you ? You must be a fool; and so I went into my box again and warmed myself, as I was almost frozen standing outside so long."

CHAPTER VIII.

A BOTTLE OF HOCK.

IT is the custom in Russia, upon undertaking a journey by road, for the traveller to provide himself with some refreshment, as it would hardly be safe to trust to the village post-houses to supply a luncheon or dinner.

On one occasion I happened to be on a road in the Government of Nishny Novgorod; my butler had provided us with a good luncheon, amongst which I knew he had placed a bottle of hock.

After proceeding on our way past two changes of horses, we came to one of those small, delightful dells which are sometimes to be found in a

Russian forest, where the diversity of the foliage affords a temporary relief to the eye from the continued appearance of the everlasting pine-tree, and where the water, gently flowing by, makes that delightful trickling murmur so grateful to hear in a country in which, as a rule, there is no sound to disturb the stillness of the steppe.

Alighting on a sunny bank, and having made a sort of nest amongst the long grass, we hoped, under the shadow of the sheltering birch-tree at our back, to enjoy our lunch, whilst I, feeling very hot and thirsty, was thinking of the hock, which I intended to cool in the stream.

The servant produced the viands, but, alas! the hock was missing! Where was it? It must have been left behind at the last post-house, the man said, as he remembered having re-arranged the seats in the tarantass, and for that purpose, had taken the luggage out of the vehicle.

So we made the best of a bad job, and enjoyed our meal without the wine.

*   *   *   *   *

A short time afterwards I was upon the same road, and thought I would find out whether my man had really left the wine behind or drunk it himself; the latter event, had the wine been sweeter than hock, might very likely have happened.

Addressing the starosta at the post-house, I demanded of him: "Ivan, did I leave a bottle behind me the last time I came through?" No; he had seen none.

I replied that it was of no particular consequence, it only being a bottle of nasty sour stuff, which, having afterwards missed from the tarantass, I was afraid I might have left behind at his station, and the idea that I had done so had made me somewhat nervous, as, whoever might have happened to drink it would experience disagreeable results,—viz., the teeth of that man would be sure to fall out afterwards.

The starosta first gave a little grin, and then evidently did not feel at his ease, in spite of his attempt to be hilarious.

I went into the house to drink a glass of tea; and on returning to the carriage, the man had become very pale and nervous, and at the moment of starting, approached me, saying, in a whisper,

"Barrin, is it really true—will my teeth come out?" "Look at mine," I replied, "and you will see;" at the same time opening my mouth, and showing him that some of mine had already disappeared.

The man gave the usual shrug, and went in-doors; but I do not think in future he will ever drink hock.

CHAPTER IX.

THE DEVIL APPEARS IN THE MINES.

SOME writers on Russia have expended much praise on the religious enthusiasm of the Russian peasant, which they have made to appear something noble, or at least respectable. I am very sorry to be obliged to declare that it is nothing of the sort: that it has very little more claim, in fact, to the name of Christianity than the fetish worship of an African tribe.

To describe the spiritual condition of these simple-hearted "mujiks," one should invert the clause of our Catechism, and, renouncing the Articles of the Christian faith, *believe* in the

Devil and all his works. I cannot illustrate the truth of my statement better than by recounting the following anecdote.

For some years, my lot compelled me to live in the interior of Russia, our establishment being one of those centres of industrial enterprise which, for their vastness, as I have already mentioned, have never been equalled.

The peasants—some forty thousand—under my charge were, perhaps, slightly above the average of their compeers in intelligence; it need not, therefore, be supposed that this story conveys an exaggerated idea of the character of the Russian mujik.

Sitting in my study one autumn afternoon, the servant announced a miner, as particularly wishing to see me. Now, for a peasant to demand an interview with his *Russian* master, especially when the latter had just dined, was a proceeding of very rare occurrence, and showed that something extraordinary must be in the wind, the distance between the native master and the mujik being very great indeed in the eyes of the former.

I, on the contrary, had found, by listening to all my men had to say, and bearing with their little weaknesses, that I found the way to their hearts, and recognized too the fact that, in some cases, the mujik is a better man than his late *owner*.

"Let him in, John," I said.

The peasant entered, looked first around him, then under the table—all the time nervously clutching at the cap he held in his hand. He literally shook in his bark shoes: his face was pale and looked all the paler by contrast with his dark eyes starting from under their eyelids.

"Barrin, I have seen the Devil!" came hoarsely whispered from his chattering lips.

"Where?" I replied.

"Oh! we have got him all right: he is down at the bottom of an ore-pit in our village; and," added he, in rather a more confident tone, "he can't get out,—the whole village have surrounded the pit."

"All right, Ivan," I said; "we will go and catch him!"

Ordering three fast horses to be put to my

tarantass, and priming my messenger with a couple of glasses of spirit to shake his be-numbed faculties together, away we went, at the rate of twenty versts an hour, to the village.

It would have been perfectly useless for me to attempt to persuade this man that the "party," whoever *he*, or whatever *it* was they had got in the pit, was not Old Nick himself. No ; the only way to convince a Russian, is to prove the matter ; and the absolute proof is not always convincing.

On my arrival at the village, I at once observed something very unusual was exciting the attention of the inhabitants, as, instead of the usual number of lazy men and women who are to bo seen standing idling about in the streets of every hamlet, I found the place deserted ; but on the neighbouring hill stood the cause of the commotion.

A crowd of people—men, women, and children, were standing around an ore-pit, some ten fathoms deep, and about as much like an ordi-nary English well, without the brick lining, as it is possible to conceive. All were talking at once (not, it may be said, quite a Russian peculiarity!), and all agreed that they had caught Old Nick himself, as they felt quite sure that the miner, who had last come out of the pit, could not possibly be mistaken.

Now came the weighty questions: "How shall we get the Devil out of his retreat? and who would boldly face the risk of tackling such an awkward customer?"

The only manner of being hoisted up and down these antiquated examples of mining, is by sitting astride a small piece of wood, fastened to the end of a not too thick piece of rope which, in its turn, is wound up and down by a wooden windlass,—not a very desirable mode of descending, even when the men are not sure the "Old Gentleman" is in their neighbourhood, but decidedly dangerous when they think he is.

I therefore declined the honour of descending; and looking about for a substitute, caught one of those rough-and-ready ne'er-do-weels, who are to be found in Russia as well as in every other country,—men who come to the surface of society

when some particular, daring deed has to be
done, and sink out of sight again when the
rewards of success have been distributed.

A few glasses of " vodka " in advance, and
three silver roubles in prospective, assisted by
friendly pats on the back by his companions,
who were afraid to go themselves, were sufficient
encouragements to animate this man of valour
to the heroic pitch.

The villagers set him astride the piece of
wood, and began to lower away.

They were in such a hurry to send him down
to the Devil, that I began to fear he would be
dropped altogether.

However, he arrived at the bottom in safety;
and now was the opportunity for observing,
more clearly and closely, how the diabolic idea
had seized on the popular mind.

All were in a rampant state of expectation.
The mayor was wondering where he could lock
up the infernal - prisoner ; in fact, doubting
whether or no he should send to the nearest
town for the assistance of the military. Two
or three suggested that I had made a mistake

in not ordering the fire-engines to come; and
many more were speculating upon the probability of their envoy having been already devoured
by the Devil.

Presently the rope shakes, which is the signal
to " hoist up." Very gently and very nervously
this operation commences. A good many of the
crowd now show signs of running away; the
men at the windlass maintain it turns very
heavily; a few peaceable citizens suggest that,
after all, perhaps the better way would be not
to bring the prisoner up, but to leave him where
he is, with a strong guard always on watch to
see that he did not pop up suddenly, and set
fire to the village; but, seeing that all this
means letting go the windlass and the poor
fellow that is attached to it, I insist on their
proceeding with the winding-up.

In time the man's head appeared, coming out
of the darkness, and he called out, " I have got
him all right ! "

The peasants then began to think that, after
all, his diabolic majesty was not so awful as they
supposed,—the captive brought to light proving

to be an immense specimen of the Horned Owl
of the Oural Mountains, whose enormous eyes
shone from his ruffled plumage like two balls
of fire.

The disappointment was very real, as, by the
time the affair had finished, the news having
spread, people were arriving from the neighbouring villages to see the wonderful sight;
and, as there was no Devil after all, the mujiks
did not think it advisable to ask me to stand
vodka all round, which, in Russia, is a natural
adjunct to the occurrence of anything extraordinary in a village.

But, perhaps, the greatest disappointment was
felt by the poor fellow who made the adven-
turous descent. He, of course, received his three
roubles, but he lost the "kudos" for his act
of daring.

In answer to the question: "Well, Ivan,
how did you manage it all?" he replied:
"Well, you see, when I got to the bottom, I
saw a something blazing; so I shut my eyes,
made a rush at it, and brought it up in my
arms in the best way I could, and here he is."

This same owl—a splendid specimen—I had stuffed, and kept facing my writing-table long afterwards, as a memento of the Russian peasants' belief in the " Devil and all his works."

CHAPTER X.

FAITH IN PRECEDENTS.

THE faith which the Russians have in precedents is remarkable.

No woman will bathe before a fixed day in June. Her belief is that on that day the water is warm enough, and will not hurt her. It may happen to be as cold as ice; but that will not prevent her taking a bath.

No man dare touch an apple before the feast of the Transfiguration, on the 6th of August, however ripe that fruit may really be before this day comes round: his creed tells him the fruit is not ready.

The village sportsman, although he may have

observed the black-cocks fighting amongst themselves unusually early, owing to the warmth of the spring, cannot make up his mind to commence the battue until the appointed day has arrived.

No traveller will start on a journey on either a Monday or a Friday.

Although strongly against his own interests, the fisherman finds it useless to cast his net before a certain day, whether the season be late or early.

No lamb is supposed to be able to reach the age of mutton should it have been born before the day named in the peasant's calendar.

According to the idea in the mind of the peasant mother, her child can only be weaned on two days in the whole year—one in July, one in January.

And so on through all the common events in their daily life does this horrible belief in precedent hedge in and surround the Russians' existence.

They are extremely pig-headed in this respect, as the incident below shows :—

I went one morning to one of our mines, where I had just placed some miners, believing we should find some very fine ore. On my arrival I came upon a' hole already opened, and could see, from the sort of clay the men were then sending up, that immediately underneath it the fine ore I was in search of would be found.

The peasants thought differently; and as they were working piece-work, bewailed their luck which had allowed them to work so long without finding ore, showing me this peculiar clay as a convincing proof that there was no ore in it.

I argued the point with them: they quickly replied, " Now look here, Barrin: we have been ore-diggers all our lives, and our fathers before us—is it likely you can know as well as we do ? and we say wherever this sort of clay is found no ore is near it."

I hinted to them that perhaps superior knowledge might have something to do with deciding the point; but that view of the question they would not listen to, and I then proposed to them that they should recommence digging upon the following terms—that if they

did not find ore I would give them a drink, whilst
if they did find the mineral they should give
me an opportunity of drinking their healths.

This suited their ideas exactly, and away they
set to work.

The next morning the chief of the gang came
to see me, and after looking about the room
and under the table, to see that nobody was
listening to his secrets, he brought out of his
pocket a piece of fine ore, and said, " Barrin,
you were right after all—the ore was there sure
enough ; " and added, " What fools we have been
to think we knew so much !—but it all comes
from our putting such faith in what has been
told us, and sticking to our old ideas."

I reversed the wager by standing a drink all
round.

This man rapidly rose in our service, and
turned out to be one of the most intelligent
men I ever had to work for me.

THE BEEKEEPER'S HOME.

CHAPTER XI.

A FOREST FIRE.

THE forests in Russia are still in many parts of enormous extent, and, owing to the scarcity of the population, have been left untouched by the axe.

I have many and many a time mounted the highest hills, and looking as far as the eye could reach, seen nothing but thickly-timbered woods covering the hills and valleys—not only dreary-looking pine-trees, but oak and elm, cedar and larch, mingling with the charming silver birch.

These forests extend for verst upon verst with hardly a single interruption. In many instances, for hundreds upon hundreds of miles, nothing is found amongst them to change the monotony of the everlasting wood, but the solitary habitation of the bee-keeper, who, without permission or payment of any sort to any one, has established himself and his hives in the midst of these solitudes. He sees no one, nor speaks to a living soul excepting on the rare occasions when he plods his way to the distant village to obtain his perhaps half-yearly supply of flour. The only stranger that ever visits him is some straying bear, who, tempted by the smell of the honey, pays him an unwelcome visit, and very soon demolishes the produce of a year.

It is during the wanderings of these peasant bee-keepers, that many of those fires arise which have done so much harm to the Russian forests.

The first thing a mujik does when stopping to rest himself after a tramp, upon his journey, is invariably to light a fire. For is he not a great believer in spirits? and besides keeping the bears away from him, the fires will help to protect him from the goblins, which he fancies hover around his leafy bed.

A thing he never does when arousing himself from his state of lethargy, to continue his solitary march, is to extinguish his fire.

The wind rises and the mischief is soon done.

The vegetation, dried and parched by the consuming sun, rapidly sucks up the fire, which spreads with a rapidity difficult to believe.

In a few moments acres of wood will be in a blaze, which fanned by the wind soon increases to miles.

In the summer season not only is the underwood as dry as touchwood, but the very ground itself is scorched up and inflammable. There is a great deal of peat in it, and this falls an easy prey to the flames, so that the earth itself igniting, the spread of the fire is fiercer and more rapid than ever.

The smoke by its denseness warns all inhabitants in the distance, of the disaster they have to expect; but little heed is paid by them to this warning : the usual shrug is the only notice taken of an event which will probably be their ruin.

For miles and miles the conflagration spreads, almost whole Governments are alight, and still nothing is done to arrest the flames, which present a glorious and magnificently grand spectacle.

Amidst the roaring of the flames and crackling of the branches stand out in bold relief, owing to the grand illumination, vast trees, perfect giants of the forest, which even this terrible fire is powerless to destroy.

The wild animals rush by before the eyes of the lookers-on, in a vain endeavour to escape from the heat following upon their heels. The large birds scream with fright, as, suffocated with the smoke, they tumble into the burning mass. Hares are seen sitting still from horror, and the small birds cease their song.

As now and then the flames reach some small hoard of dried wood, laid up for the peasant's winter store, the fire appears to receive a fresh impetus, and raging more fearfully than before, spreads with a fierceness which seems as if nothing could restrain or check.

Villages at length are reached, and come down like tinder : the outlying little homesteads only offer fresh fuel, whilst the small stacks of hay and corn, the mujik's " little all," are burned the moment they are reached.

Finally towns become threatened, and that causes a little stir to be made. The local Governor grows nervous, and thinks he would have done well to have interfered before; the mayors of the burned-down villages are summoned for information, and abused for not having extinguished the conflagration ; the fire-engines are inspected, and found out of order ; the water-carts are leaky, and the brigade generally useless; but something must be done, or the Emperor will hear of it, and a commission be sent down, which will probably turn everybody out of office from the Governor down to the starosta.

Then comes the opportunity for the mujik to exercise his ingenuity. All the available men from the neighbourhood of the fire are told off, under the command of one of the local mayors, and then proceed to their work, provided with hatchets and spades. A certain number of the men follow one another with their axes in hand, chopping a line in the ground, in such a manner as to encircle the fire; they again are followed by the remainder of the party, who, with spades, just throw aside the earth turned up from the line. This illiputian ditch is sufficient to check the flames and their devastation, as in these sort of fires it is the grass and underwood that spread the enemy.

These conflagrations are sometimes tremendous in their extent : the last one of great importance was in 1869, which, commencing in the Government of Tver, spread until it reached nearly to Wilna, in the centre of Poland.

CHAPTER XII.

THE MUJIK'S WAY OF BEGGING.

A RUSSIAN mujik never comes to his master and asks straight out for what he wants. There must be a deal of circumlocution first, before the " Barrin " knows what the man really wants. I can give no reason for, or explanation of, this custom, but illustrate the fact by recording one of the many instances that occurred within my knowledge.

A man entered my room, dressed in his best; he asked kindly after my own health and that of my family, began fidgeting with his cap, and said, " Barrin, can you give me a few timbers, as I am building a new house ? " " How many do you want, Gabriel ?" I asked. "As many as you will be pleased to give me," he replied. "Will twenty be enough?" "Certainly," the man answered. "Well, all right," I said. "Tell Nicolai Ivanovitch to give you an order to receive them." With a "Very much obliged to you—good morning, Excellency," Gabriel went out of the room, apparently well satisfied.

In a couple of moments he returned, poked his head just inside the doorway, and said, " Barrin, it is not wood I want, but bricks." "Well, how many do you want?" I asked. "Two cartloads." "All right ; go and take them," I told him. Then I knew he was satisfied, and had got what he wanted; for he came up to me and kissed the sleeve of my coat.

He would have tumbled on his knees and kissed my boots ; but this abjectness is detestable to foreigners, and as the mujiks must be allowed to carry out their predilections to a certain extent for their own satisfaction, I met them in this manner halfway by holding out my hand.

CHAPTER XIII.

TRADE UNIONS AND STRIKES.

TRADE unions and strikes are not indigenous to the United Kingdom: we have them in Russia, the latter very frequently.

Concerning the Russian workman, it has been written: "I have found frequently that the Russians were amongst the best workmen to be found in any country. I do not mean that a Russian can do anything like the same quantity of work that an Englishman can, but he can imitate anything. Give him a model to be precisely reproduced, and he will produce it, whatever it is, from a padlock to a watch."

No one, however, understands a "strike" better than a Russian workman. I say workman, in contradistinction to a common agricultural peasant.

On the emancipation of the serfs, in 1861, it was only the ordinary mújiks who received land from their late proprietors. The "mistarovoys," or workmen attached to all the great works, were not regarded in the same light, and the majority of those attached to the works in the centre of Russia are without land. I can mention one circumstance to prove the oddness of the ideas held by some of the serfs upon this question. A proprietor of one of the largest of these works at the time of the emancipation, offered to let any of his workmen have land on the same terms as the other mujiks, but only the men from one of his twelve zavods accepted this liberal offer.

The workmen received their garden-ground to the extent of one deciatine, but did not participate in the agricultural land.

They have no voice in the communal questions of division of the land, and do not take much interest in the affairs of the village generally. In consequence of having no "obrok" to pay for the land, they, too, are free to go "abroad" to search for work.

A Russian leaving his own village to seek for work, is always said to have gone "abroad," whilst a man from a neighbouring property is designated as a "foreigner."

It is the "mistarovoys" who puddle the iron, roll the sheets, and forge the nails, whilst the ordinary mujiks burn the charcoal, cut the wood, dig the ore, &c.; and before any common peasant can become a "mistarovoy," he must go through a course of learning his trade.

Russians give no notice of strikes. Some gabbler amongst the men puts into their heads the idea that they can earn more money at a neighbouring works, and as a result on Monday morning the men do not put in an appearance. It is never any use arguing with them; the only way is to make them suffer, and when they begin to get hungry they come to work again.

In the unions which they have amongst themselves they have laws respecting their work;

such regulations as the apportionment of pay between master, workman, and journeyman; the time a man must serve as a journeyman before he can call himself a master; the days which must be kept as holidays, and upon which it is impossible to get them to work; the appointment of a starosta; to fix the amount of waste and other trade allowances; in fact, generally, to make all rules for their own government. There is, however, a great difference between their unions and those in England. In Russia all the executive work gratuitously, and the unions, as far as I know, never subscribe anything to keep their brethren who may be on strike.

A Russian strike is never caused from any calculations as to cost and sale, or as to whether the master can afford to pay any increase of wages, but simply from the desire to obtain a little more money to spend in vodka; for the workman drinks much more than the common peasant.

The laws affecting works in Russia are in such an unsatisfactory state, that many excuses can be made for the men striking. By an old statute, which ought to have been repealed when the Emancipation Act was passed, every proprietor is compelled to feed his workmen, whether they are employed or not; this, then, is a great incentive to laziness, although I do not mean to say that this law is strictly enforced. But it is a curious fact, and must have been the result of an oversight, that whilst the workman became a free man, and could take his labour where he pleased, the master was not freed from the obligations he incurred towards his people when they were serfs.

But the strikes in Russia are as nothing compared to the combinations with which an employer of labour is assailed by his men.

For example, the supply of ore at the furnace mouth is observed to be getting low; the peasants immediately demand more money for digging and carting. Charcoal, too, is short; the "Barrin" is informed that the roads are so bad, an increased rate must be paid for the carriage; in fact, it is not a comfortable thing to be in the mujiks' hands then.

One of the most noted and curious of these cases occurred amongst the peasants of a village in the Government of Vladimir, and I cannot resist quoting it, in order to show how these combinations arise, and the best manner of checking them.

In certain works it was necessary to introduce gas, both for the purposes of economy, and to afford an improved light.

The gasworks were built, and contracts entered into with the mujiks for the supply of birch-bark, as in Russia the outside of the birch-tree is very generally used for the purpose of making gas.

The works were brilliantly illuminated, but the opportunity was too good a one for the peasants to let slip through their fingers, and this was what they said amongst themselves :—

" Now, if we all make an arrangement not to carry any more bark under thirty copecks a pood [they were then receiving fifteen copecks a pood, a magnificent rate of pay], the 'Barrin' must give in to us, as he has thrown all the old lamps

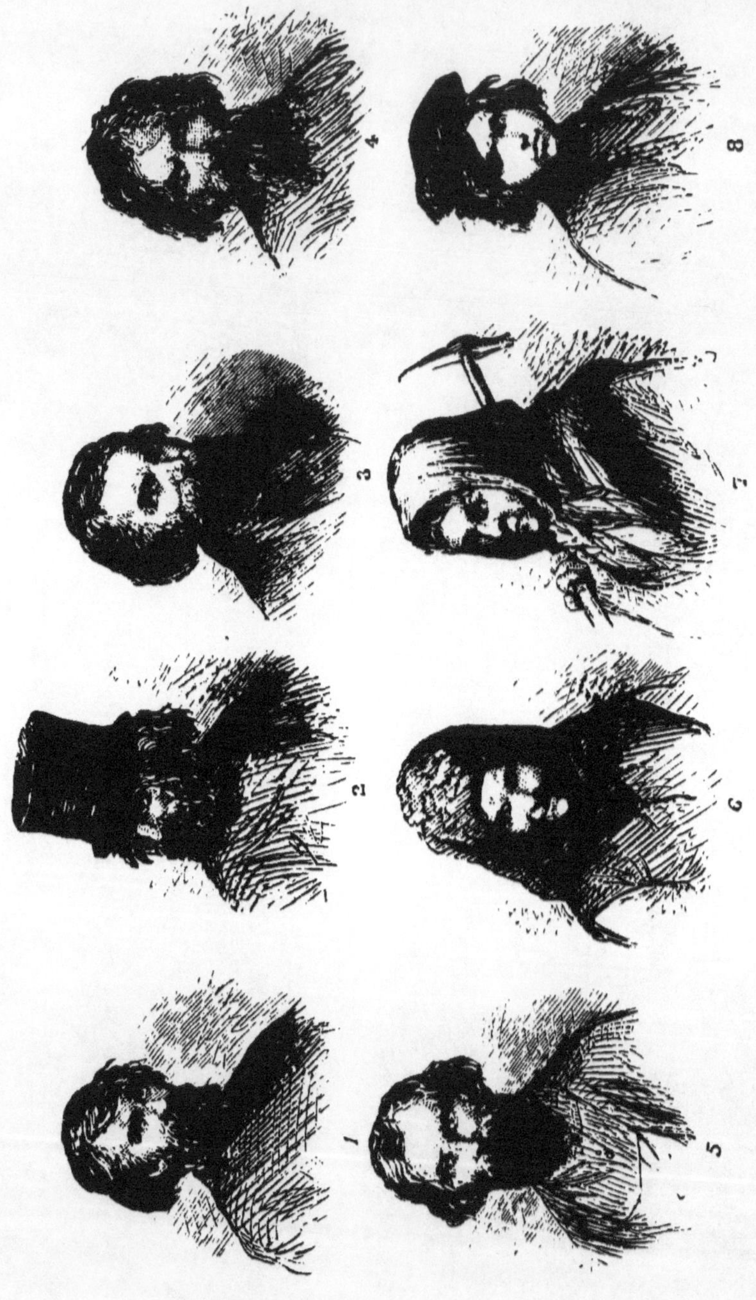

away, and cannot light the works without our bark."

This goodly company adjourned to the traktir, and amidst much vodka-drinking, much swearing, and a great deal of crossing before the saintly pictures, the little plot was arranged.

The director received the demands of his men apparently with great civility, and immediately fell into their views as to price; for his orders were heavy, and darkness would have ruined him.

The mujiks were delighted with the success of their little trick — they were beside themselves with joy; for not only had the director not sworn at them, but he had not paid them out by any of those little means at his disposal—such as stopping their cattle going into the woods, forbidding them to fish in the streams, &c., and they bethought themselves of again putting up the price to their complacent friend.

The mistake they had made will be found in the sequel.

One morning the works were full of carts, they lined the road for versts; in fact, reached almost to the river, where report said barges upon barges had arrived, loaded with the same curious-looking black stone as was then being discharged in the yard. "What was this stuff?" was asked from mouth to mouth amongst the peasants. Anyhow, it did not much matter to them; for it was clearly not bark, and they increased their efforts to double the size of the stacks before their houses, anticipating the fresh demands they intended making.

The director was in no hurry to discover himself; for he foresaw a good profit to the works in all these accumulated stores of an article that was really a necessity to him.

In time, the barges were all unloaded—the last lump was added to the pile, and then the director proceeded to calculate how much this cargo of cannel coal had cost him; for it was by making the mujiks recoup him all this expense, that he intended to pay out these clever fellows.

A very heavy debit it was. The coal was brought out from England to St. Petersburg, in a steam-ship, sent by railway to Moscow, and from thence two hundred miles by water and land carriage. However the director had made his plans and carried them out in the following manner.

Assembling them all before the coal he thus addressed them :—

" *Now*, you blackguards, what is the price of your bark ? Do you know what that stuff is you are looking at ? It is coal, fine coal, coal full of gas ! Your bark is rubbish, and makes bad gas, so I have sent to England to get this coal out; and now I will show you what gas is. What is the price of your bark now ? Get out, you pigs, I have done with you."

The neighbouring traktir soon saw the mujiks discussing the matter. " What a clever fellow Ivan Ivanovitch is," said one, " to get all that stone together in order to try and frighten us; but it won't do," and with a drunken laugh added, " You can't make gas out of stones. Ah ! ah ! "

Reeling back to the office they assailed the director with the same impudent demands, and stoutly refused to abate the price one iota.

Ivan Ivanovitch refused to take any more of the bark, but that did not open their eyes.

" He has had a quantity of his gas kept in reserve," they declared, " and thinks to frighten us, but we will see what ho says in a few days."

Some weeks passed by and still gas was seen burning. The mujiks at length began to believe there must be some truth in the coal story after all, and so one by one the bark dealers arrived to inform the director that after all they had been playing with him. " We would not charge you too dear for bark, not we !" exclaimed these repentant and frightened extortionists.

Ivan Ivanovitch had nothing to say to them for a long time, in fact, until about half his stock of coal was exhausted, then he began to deal with them, and finally knocked the price down for future supplies from fifteen copecks a pood, which was the price he had originally paid, to ten copecks for the same weight; and in order to guard against further combinations of the same sort, he kept the remaining stock of coal unused in the yard. Since that time he has never been troubled with combinations.

CHAPTER XIV.

THE CORONER.

GOSPODIN Ivan Volkoff was a dandy, dressed very smartly, always appeared with tight kid gloves on his hands, and, moreover, was the only man in the village who possessed a chimneypot hat, which he wore on all state occasions.

Report said, too, that he lived well, never fasted, and drank the best of wines.

That he must have been a clever man, in spite of my belief to the contrary, is proved by the fact that he did all the above on a salary of one hundred and twenty pounds a year, one hundred of which was stopped by the local treasury to pay his old debts.

The business of the coroner was to hold inquests or preliminary inquiries in cases of theft, robbery, &c., and so to speak, get up the case for the local judge. It consequently depended very much upon the report this functionary made as to whether the verdict would be " guilty " or " not guilty."

No wonder, then, that in a place where thefts were very frequent and justice very slow, Gospodin Volkoff made a decent income. His price was not heavy. If a man had ten roubles he took it, if only three he was contented with that; and people said that he had been known to accept as small a present as one rouble, or the equivalent to our half-crown.

He wore a uniform, and sitting at his judicial table with black coat, green velvet collar and gold eagled buttons, he overawed the mujiks with his grand appearance.

All his business was written; for instance, in examining a witness, the questions which he was to answer were all handed to him written on a

sheet of paper, with a margin left for the answer
to be written against the questions.

As three-quarters of the witnesses examined
could neither read nor write, it was not a very
difficult thing 'for the coroner to get what
answers he wished out of them; for he wrote
these answers for them, and the witness placed
his three crosses at the bottom of the paper, as
his acceptance of the truth of what, through his
own ignorance, he knew nothing about.

Some of these papers were wonderful examples
of ingenuity; as when some unfortunate individual got into Gospodin Volkoff's hands who
could not pay the usual fee, the way the man
was proven to have sworn black was white, and
white was black, was wonderful; for the coroner
examined the accuser, as well as the witnesses,
in the case.

A few of these reports of his were great
curiosities in their way.

A peasant had stolen some iron, and was
caught red-handed. The report on the case
stated that the iron had never been stolen at
all, but had been eaten up with rust.

Staves were continually being made away with by the miners, who were, at last, caught taking them home to burn. The report on this case was, that the rain had washed the staves away.

A small proprietor had lost his watch, which was found on a mujik, who could give no satisfactory account of how he became possessed of it. The inquest found that it had been dropped down the peasant's chimney by the owner himself!

Some bank-notes were stolen, which were found in a man's house, and proved to be those lost. The intelligent coroner reported that the notes were all forged ones, and therefore the case could not proceed.

And so the coroner went merrily on, enjoying himself, and drinking his champagne.

But his time came at last. One day, he was caught in the act of passing away some forged notes, which, it was clearly proved, formed part of a lot he had bought cheap from the manufacturer; and thus the society of this valuable servant of the Crown was lost to the village.

He was succeeded by a fool, but still an honest one; and then all the people grumbled at *him*, saying they preferred a knave to a fool; but at last we got the benefit of the new law, and that gave us a justice of the peace, and honesty.

CHAPTER XV.

FATALISM.

RUSSIANS are all fatalists. In every rank of society this is the case.

I was called to a fire at a village, and, by the time I arrived there, the whole place was burned clean down, with the exception of the church and Gospotsky Dom. The village did not belong to us, as we had only hired it. On nearing the house, I noticed all the furniture moved out into the garden, and the steward, wrapped up in ever so many great-coats, sitting upon a heap of it, with an immense horse-pistol in his arms. I thought the fire had been too much for his nerves, and that the man was mad.

"Hullo! Ystimoff!" I said, "What is the matter?—why don't you put the furniture into the house again? The fire is all over."

"No," he said; "I'm afraid;" and added, "the house is sure to be burned!"

"Why?" I asked; and this is what he recounted to me:—

"I was going for a ride in the wood, the other day, when I met an old woman, who told me that the village was going to be burned down, because she had just met on the road a man, who had escaped from prison, who belonged to the village, and that whenever such an escaped prisoner came to his native village, it was sure to be burned down. I asked her, as the Gospotsky Dom was a little way from the village, whether that would be burned down too, and she said that it would. Now, as she has so far shown herself to be right, I am quite sure that our house will be burned: and so I shall keep the furniture out of doors, in order to save it."

I could not reason him out of his ideas; but the fire never came, and the house stands to-day. Whether Ystimoff's master thought his furniture had been saved by being exposed to the rain for a week, I do not know.

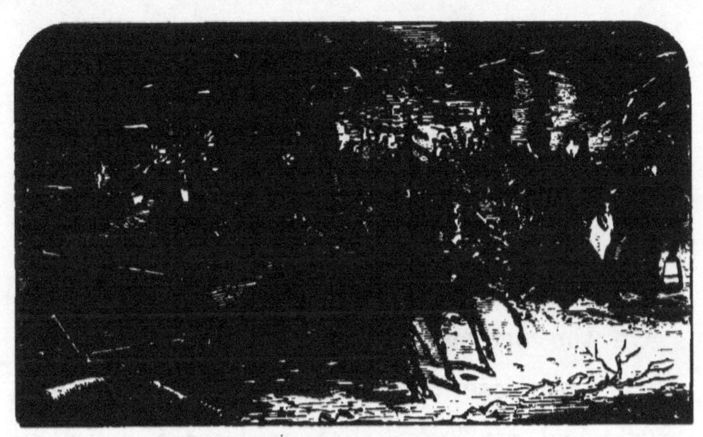

CHAPTER XVI.

A NARROW ESCAPE.

BUSINESS compelled me to drive across a large extent of steppe country, that flat, dreary, snow-covered plain, which has not one single object for miles and miles to attract the eye, or to give the slightest relief from the whiteness of the snow, which, after a time, fairly dazzles one with its unceasing glitter.

The peculiar stillness that reigns in the atmosphere is at such times most depressing—

everything appears literally dead, and the echo of one's horses' bells comes rushing back in a weird and gloomy manner, as though it were impossible to escape from the scene.

On the occasion I am describing, at a time when I suppose we must have been near some brushwood, we heard that unpleasant half-yelp, half-bark, which warns the traveller that the wolf is not only about, but also on the hunt; and although then there is not the slightest danger, as a wolf must be very hungry indeed before he attacks a sledge, still the noise is not comfortable, and makes one, instead of enjoying a pleasant sleep, to be continually feeling whether the pistol is safe in the holster.

The following day, as we were getting out of the steppe country, and reaching the waste, covered with stunted birch-trees and shrubs, that always succeed it, I shut my eyes, and, having been in the sledge for several days, and very fatigued, slept on, quite unconscious of the bumps and rolls.

Night came on; and when I woke up, I could see we had strayed off the road, and, what was

worse, there was no finding it again. I calculated we were many, many miles from our proper
route; and, having given the man instructions
to drive by the stars, went to sleep again, as
the best means of passing the hour or two
before reaching a road I should know something
about.

Presently, the man turned round, began
poking me with his whip, and cried out,
" Wolves !—wolves ! Barrin ! Shoot—for God's
sake, be quick ! "

I jumped up, took out my pistol, and leant
over the man to look for the wolves. I could
not see any; but being only half-awake, asked
the man where the wolves were.

He was by this time very frightened, and shook
all over, as he said, " There, there !—shoot,
shoot quickly ! " at the same time pointing to a
light, which I now perceived a little way ahead
of us amongst the bushes.

A second afterwards, I saw that this glimmer
was a lantern, and immediately the bearer of it
emerged from the bushes—a woman, leading her
drunken husband along.

I said to the driver, "Why, what an ass you must be! Waking up, as I did, so suddenly from my sleep, I might, as likely as possible, have shot where you pointed to, and killed somebody! What made you think that it was a wolf?"

"Well, you see," he said, "I have never seen a wolf myself, but I have heard that their eyes are like fire; and, therefore, seeing a light in the wood, I naturally thought that it must be a wolf, and so I cried out."

CHAPTER XVII.

OUR VILLAGE SHOPS.

A VILLAGE, a thousand miles from St. Petersburg, had a population of about four thousand people, and attracted many visitors, both for pleasure and business; so that the shops were really worthy of the name.

The principal portion of them were situated in one row, and consisted of five shops. Number one was kept by a German, who, on account of his nationality, did not do a large business, confining his attention to vending such trifles as charms, steel pens, photographs, &c. Number two was a large linen-draper's, where the assortment of prints was far superior to anything to be seen in a country town in England ; the proprietor of this establishment also dealt in silks and satins, shawls and velvets. Number three was a grocer's, with all sorts of commodities expected to be found in such an establishment; whilst number four was the most original of all the shops : it was kept by one Feodor, who spent the greater part of the year in hawking over the country, only honouring us with his presence during some three months of the year. His stock consisted of buttons, trimmings, tapes, braid, and such small articles as are very necessary for ladies' use, and so the ladies of our house were constantly paying Feodor a visit in his hybernating season.

Now, Feodor was like the bears in winter. He loved sleep, and determined to take it; so all day long he might be seen lying on an iron bedstead by his counter, fast asleep. His small boy and assistant kept watch and ward; and on the appearance of his customers, with a "Feodor Ivanovitch, here are the ladies," shook his master, who, after many attempts, rising from the folds of his sheepskin coat, with a simultaneous yawn and rub of the eyes, crawled on to the counter from his nest, and scrambled over it as well as he could, prepared to attend on the ladies, and with his " Madushka " (my little mother) manner of addressing them, was a stiff hand at a bargain.

Last, but by no means least, came number five, the shop of Mr. Nikepatmikof. He was a general dealer, blending concerns similar to Fortnum & Mason's with the Lowther Arcade and Copeland's. Few things could be asked for, with which Nikepatmikof could not supply you. His truffles were first-rate; his Rœderer was genuine; his cigars were veritable *ne plus ultra* of Uppman's; but this old fellow had one weakness —he was fond of money, and, consequently, was continually raising his prices without the slightest regard to the state of the market: so at last I had to grant a licence for an opposition shop to open; and thus by a little healthy competition, we got what we wanted—fair prices.

All these shops were raised above the road by a wooden platform, which was covered in; here the proprietors amused themselves, whiling away the time with the usual tea-drinking and draught-playing, whilst their assistants were principally occupied hanging round the entrance of their neighbours' shops, seeing what business they were doing, and watching the customers making their purchases.

We had a few other shops about the village, and altogether I know of no article of ordinary use that could not be obtained.

We had tailors and dressmakers, not by any means ordinary ones, but such as were capable of making clothes for anybody, were he Prince. or Princess.

We had photographers, who, if they were not artists, understood their business; and it is from their labours that some of the illustrations of this book have been taken.

CHAPTER XVIII.

A HURRICANE.

THE climate of Russia exhibits some anoma-
lies which it is very difficult to account for.
Hurricanes are by no means uncommon. Let
me attempt to describe one.

Sitting in the balcony on one of the early days
of May, enjoying that calmness and serenity in the
atmosphere which is one of the peculiar features
of the Russian climate; refreshing myself with
occasional glances at the greenness of the grass
which had only just been allowed, through the
disappearance of the snow, to show its face; I
thought of the long, cold, dreary winter just
passed away, and of the enjoyment to be expected
from the coming summer.

In the park the starlings, on their flight of passage, were resting on the budding sprigs of the lime-trees.

The leafy woods in the distance were full of hares jumping and toying with the now peeping branches of the undergrowth; the game-birds were cooing and fighting with delight at the arrival of spring-time; and the butterflies were trying to eclipse the beauty of the wild flowers just emerging from their mossy bed.

The lake was so calm and quiet that it was not impossible to believe the ancient country legend of the maiden who saw her lover, though far away, depicted on the surface of the water; in fact, the stillness of everything was almost painful.

In one moment all this scene was changed. The sky suddenly became overcast, day seemed to have changed into night, the thunder roared and roared again, the wind blew with a force frightening to behold, a cloud of sand and dust rose which eddied in circles upon circles, each trying to overtake another.

Rain poured down as though in verity the

heavens were opened and the world about to be drowned again. The wind, meanwhile, burst into perfect fury—seized upon trees which had stood the ravages of time for centuries, snapping them asunder as though they were but reeds.

The waves of the lake lashed themselves into a veritable sea ; the waters, dashed into spray and foam, were thrown with such force against the dams which should keep them back, that these works, which took thousands of men ages to achieve, were threatened with destruction.

Roofs of houses might be seen sailing over the plain : furnaces built to withstand all changes in the weather, and thus ponderously strong, went down before the ruthless wind as though they were built of paper : the whole country was a sea of water : the roar of the engines was drowned by the rattle of the hail-stones.

In the works, iron, charcoal, wood, and machinery were blowing about in one confused mass; all the elements seemed at war one with another.

The very horses in the stables were scared, and huddled together shaking with fear. The fowls all went to roost; the ducks and geese were not to be seen; the small birds flew into the houses for shelter; and the pigs squealed and cried as if they were being killed.

Altogether the sight was an awful one, and not to be easily obliterated from the memory,—— and in ten minutes' time all this was changed again for serenity and sunshine.

CHAPTER XIX.

CLIMATE.

A COUNTRY so vast in extent as Russia, necessarily has many climates. This was never brought to my mind so forcibly as when viewing the Ethnographical Museum at Moscow. In this exhibition there were examples of all the peoples acknowledging the dominion of the Czar; these were so varied as to commence with·an Esquimaux, and finish with a copper-coloured fire-worshipper.

In European Russia, as well as in many parts of Siberia, the climate cannot be considered disagreeable. The winters are severe, after our notions; but in the absence of wind, the cold is not intensely felt.

About — 20° Reaumur, may be taken as a fair average of the cold; and, although — 30° will not be uncommon, even that, allowing for the extreme clearness and dryness of the atmosphere, is very supportable.

The rivers in the centre and north of Russia this side of the Oural range, generally freeze up about the same time—namely, the end of November, new style,—and open about the end of March. This is also about the time that snow ceases to fall.

Sometimes, great and sudden changes occur in the temperature during the winter months. I remember that on one day in the month of February, 1868, in the Government of Nijny Novgorod, the thermometer stood at + 5° at 12 o'clock in the morning, and, in the same night, read — 41° or a difference of 46° in sixteen hours.

From the habits of the people great precautions are invariably taken in their clothing, to protect themselves from the cold; and I never suffered from the climate in Russia, even in the severest weather, so much as I do in England.

The heat succeeds the cold weather so quickly that, whilst in the spring all vegetation is far behind our own, the harvest is gathered in much earlier than ours.

The summers are hot—at times uncomfortably so,—although there is usually a slight breeze, which takes off the heaviness of the great heat; and the evenings are, without exception, cool and a little damp, so much so in the neighbourhood of St. Petersburg as to be very dangerous to persons unaccustomed to the climate.

The climate is undoubtedly favourable to the growth of cereals and vegetables; and, if the soil in the centre of Russia were better, the productions in this respect would be remarkable.

I think one great reason of this is that, whilst the days are extremely hot, the nights, as I have before observed, are very moist. I obtained seeds of our different vegetables from England, and the size to which the produce of some of these attained was singular. The peas and beans were far superior to anything I have ever seen in England.

The interior and north of Russia are not suitable to the growth of fruit, the winters being too severe for the trees to live in the open air. For instance, cherries will not grow out of doors to any extent, farther north than Vladimir. As a result, with the exception of the wild fruits obtained in the woods, where they are very abundant, the superior sorts are all grown under glass. Some of this fruit is fine, and the Russians are probably the possessors of the largest-grown peach in the world; it is called the " Venus," and is of a magnificent colour. I have picked three peaches, weighing two pounds and a half, from off a tree of this description; they are better to look at, however, than to eat.

As is well known, fruit abounds in the south of Russia, and the apples and grapes of the Crimea are second to none in the world. About Kief, and those districts, numbers of pears grow wild, and these, dried and preserved with honey, are a very extensive article of commerce. The neighbourhood of Kief is also noted for the manufacture and preservation of all sorts of fruits and sweetmeats, the varied extent of which is not surpassed in any other part of the globe, excepting, perhaps, the islands of the South Pacific.

The south of Russia is adapted, both as regards soil and climate, for the growth of the grape. Even now, the cxltivation of the vine has achieved some importance in the neighbourhood of the Don, but, owing to ignorance of the proper method of preparing the wine, the article produced is very inferior. There seems, however, to be a great opening for any one to develop this branch of industry, and there is no reason whatever why Russia should not produce wines of a very respectable quality in very respectable quantities. One enterprising proprietor, Prince Woronzoff, has introduced into his estate in the Crimea a very proper system; the result is, that many a worse bottle of wine may be drunk in France than on this nobleman's estate.

CHAPTER XX.

" MASLINITZ " OR CARNIVAL.

THE maslinitz is ushered in with an inordinate consumption of " bleenies " or pancakes. These are eaten with fresh caviare by the better class, and with butter by the common people. When the holiday week is over, the long fast commences, only to be finished by the advent of Easter: the people therefore find it necessary to lay in a stock of solids, to make up for the dreary days of maigre living which ensue.

All sorts of distractions and amusements are provided during this week for the recreation of the people.

As is the custom in continental cities, the usual parades take place in the towns, and in the villages everybody turns out for a drive, from the Barrin in his sledge, with smart troika of horses, to the peasant in his clumsy kibitka adorned with a Siberian rug hung on the back, making at least a colourable picture, if not a pretty one.

On these occasions sliding and sledging down the ice hills are very favourite amusements, and a game resembling hockey is played on the ice. The traktirs do a flourishing business, and singing and dancing are to be seen in every street.

Two things a mujik *must* do during this week of rioting and dissipation, or he believes his stars will be unlucky—he must take one drive, and get drunk once.

Every house that possesses or can secure a musician for the occasion has its ball, and accompaniment of romps. The people pass from house to house to these entertainments without any invitation.

Dancing of all sorts goes on, from French quadrilles to the " kapalooshka " or Russian national dance, which is performed by two persons only at a time. The man, standing opposite his chosen partner, commences with a pantomimic invitation to dance, which, after much stepping and gyrating between the two, is finally accepted. Each then in turn dances some time, with the smallest of steps, seldom moving their feet off the ground; and continually swaying their arms and bodies in a by no means ungraceful style. The dance finishes by the gentleman imprinting a kiss on the lips of his now willing partner.

During the dance, when any particularly graceful step or movement is made, the spectators applaud by clapping their hands.

The games are principally confined to kiss in the ring, and an amusement very similar to our hunt the slipper.

One great feature worthy of observation at these entertainments, is the absence of all jollity. The people talk very little, and the elder folks sit round the room, looking rather depressed than otherwise, excepting when they rise, which they do pretty frequently, for the purpose of taking a schnapps.

A quantity of " koolibak," or prodigious cakes made of bread containing fish, carrots, rice or meat, together with apples and vodka, are the refreshments provided.

Many of the visitors are masked and dominoed, and many more of the females wear the national holiday costume, the sarafan or dress of which is made of some bright-coloured stuff trimmed with gold and suspended with short shoulder-straps; under this, the rubashka or large loose-sleeved shirt is worn. The hair of the unmarried girls is plaited in one plait, lengthened with many coloured ribbons; and a sort of tiara, generally ornamented with beads, adorns the head. The costume is completed by a handsomely-trimmed apron, and with the richer peasants a necklace and earrings of the largest amber beads.

All kinds of cast-off finery are used by the maskers, and uniforms of every description are borrowed for the occasion.

Should the village possess a " Gospotsky Dom," the Barrin always opens his house in honour of the time. The largest room is decorated, music is provided, and in some of the smaller chambers, refreshments of various descriptions are at the disposal of the guests.

The revels commence soon after dusk, and all night long a stream of people come and go, as it is not customary for a visitor to remain in one house all the evening.

These are really bals masqués, as almost every one comes in costume, and all the inhabitants are seen mixing together in one common crowd. Here some real fun goes on, and the dancing is fast and furious. The Tchinovnik is to be seen dancing with the work-girl, and the housemaid with the clerk. The popes look in, but do not dance, confining their attentions to the champagne and meats.

One room is set aside for smokers who wander in between the dances, and take a papiross, whilst one of the company, a mujik very probably, sings a song to the accompaniment of the piano.

The Barrin all the time moves about among his guests, with a word for each, and a welcome for all.

Some representatives of itinerant professions will probably look in during the evening, such as a bear-leader with his bear,—a wandering story-teller, — a Greek vendor of holy relics, — and last, not least, a church beggar. All will be well got up, and give a good idea of Russian customs.

During the revels where I was host, the hospitality of the master was not abused: no one got drunk, and nobody made a row. All seemed well pleased with the entertainment, and I cannot doubt that if a little more of such mixing took place amongst the classes in Russia, the aristocrats would be benefited by it.

CHAPTER XXI.

THE GOVERNOR.

I WAS frequently compelled to make a journey to the government or capital town of the district, to see our Governor on official business.

His Excellency was one of the honourable governors in Russia; that is to say, he did not take bribes and presents, and conducted the affairs of his government generally with discretion and respectability.

Of course, he lived in the Governor's house,— a large, cold, miserable-looking building, with suites of immense rooms, very barely furnished, but which, I believe, the Governor thought were magnificent. Everything in that establishment was arranged to strike awe into the minds of the visitors.

A guard was posted outside, and a second in the hall, and the way in which those Cossacks whirled about their swords on the entry of any one they supposed should be treated with more respect than usual, was sufficient to make a nervous man wince.

The Governor "received" once a week, and that was the day to see the establishment at the height of its splendour.

The anteroom was filled on those occasions with all sorts and descriptions of people. Officers in full-dress, covered with orders; civil servants in holiday attire, cocked hats and swords; local magnates from the town; a few long-coated, high-booted delegates from one or other of the smaller towns of the Government, who, with their hair highly greased, their hands encased in white kid gloves, and ponderous silver medals suspended by gaudily-coloured ribbons from the neck, did not look at all at their ease. Some village mayors, wearing their brass medals and chains of office, and a sprinkling of mujiks, made up the company.

I have often observed at those receptions, how the swaggering, bullying manner of the small local jacks-in-office had sobered down in the expected presence of the great man.

On one occasion I remember seeing an individual standing at the doorway of the anteroom, as straight and as fixed as a sentinel, dressed up in the most laughable of uniforms, something between that of a cabinet minister and a post-man. This fellow was the procureur of a small town near us, and he was in the habit of coming to our office, and behaving himself generally as a rampageous tiger. Then his deportment was humbled, and he was afraid for his very life to move a muscle.

Presently, amid general expectation, the door opened, and the great man issued from his *sanctum sanctorum*.

The general, for he was a military governor, was slightly pompous, and with his long chibook in his hand, walked amongst his audience, yelling rather than talking to the small fry.

Visitors of greater distinction were honoured with a private audience afterwards.

But to see the Governor in all his glory, some night must be chosen when he was going in state to the theatre; the "State" consisting of one solitary mounted Cossack, clattering after the general's one-horse droschky! On entering the house, he would be received amidst solemn silence, and so, bowing to this one, nodding to that, and I am bound to add, winking to another, he would slowly make his way to his seat.

No wonder, however, the general had his little weaknesses, for he had risen from the ranks, and having undergone what *that* meant in those days, could not be blamed for enjoying his hardly-earned *otium cum dignitate* when he had the chance.

Moreover, he had been a fighting general, and had obtained many steps of his rank as rewards for successfully carrying out his arduous duties as a feld-jager or bearer of despatches: he was also the hero of the following curious episode.

The Emperor Nicholas was exceedingly exacting in the demands he made upon his military couriers. They were required to travel about twelve miles an hour, and could never stop during the whole journey for more than three minutes at a time for the purpose of changing horses. The distance was nothing, the rule was inflexible. It was only a few men who could stand this sort of work, and one of them was our general.

When holding but humble military rank, he one day, as courier, dashed up to the Winter Palace in St. Petersburg. He reported himself to the aide-de-camp on duty, as the bearer of despatches from the Caucasus. The aide-de-camp immediately reported his arrival to the Emperor, who always received these important documents with his own hands.

The Emperor returned quickly to the room, where he found the courier lying on the floor, either fast asleep or insensible. The unfortunate fellow was pulled and shaken, but without any effect; overcome by the fatigue of the journey, he seemed to have sunk into a helpless lethargy.

What could be done! No man ought to sleep before the Czar, even under such circumstances;

but the Czar himself was equal to the emergency. He went up to the messenger, stooped down, and whispered in his ear, in the language of the post-house starosta, " The horses are ready, Excellency ! " " All right," shouted the now awakened courier, believing he was still on the road, " Go on and be damned " !

The man's promotion was rapid from that day.

CHAPTER XXII.

THE OLD AND THE NEW JUDGES.

I MADE the acquaintance of the former in rather a curious way.

Being at the Court in a provincial town, where I had gone to sign a " paper," my clerk found it was necessary that my identity should be proved before the judge would witness my signature. It was the first time I had ever been to the place, and as far as I knew no inhabitant had ever set eyes on me. Under the circumstances what could I do! My clerk informed me that he would soon arrange the matter, and, leaving the room, shortly reappeared with a gentleman whom I had never had the pleasure of seeing before, but who with-

out any ado, crossed himself, and said I was the
man I represented myself to be. This, of course,
settled the business, and the paper was duly
attested. A moment after, I saw from the
window my willing witness rushing down the
street in chase of my clerk, who had gone to
the inn, as the Tchinovnik knew a good dinner,
accompanied with a couple of bottles of porter,
had been ordered by the clerk for himself and
friend as a delicate·attention for his testimony.

This then was Roman Romanovitch, who at
that time occupied the position of third judge,
and who in the course of time filled the arduous
though profitable position of first judge.

His personal appearance was not in his favour.
Nature had not endowed him with much forehead,
and with his closely-cut, almost shaven hair, his
head appeared to be as round as a bullet; his
eyes were very small, and his body was very
large, and he was decidedly anything but a man
of imposing appearance. In standing he had
that peculiar habit very common amongst all
Tchinovniks, of keeping one hand in his pocket,
whilst the other, always held behind his back, was

continually opening and shutting itself with a nervous clutching motion. If not, therefore, letting the right hand know what the left was doing, it looked very much as though the left hand was feeling in the pocket for that which the right hoped to put into it.

The pay of my friend was not large, as in his position of chief judge he received from the Government three hundred roubles, or about forty pounds a year; but then he had the power of deporting people to Siberia, and that was a valuable privilege in a money-making country.

It was not to be wondered at, that with such a small salary, Roman Romanovitch could not pay that attention to dress and toilette which a man in his position might wish to do.

He wore the usual judicial uniform of dress coat with green velvet collar and brass buttons, but his trousers were of varied hue and colour, and had probably belonged to his grandfather. Linen, so far as collar went, did not trouble him much, and as he only shaved twice a week, his general appearance, say on a Tuesday afternoon, was not all that could be wished.

The fact was that Roman Romanovitch liked good living and playing at cards, so his *income*, which was not so very small, went in this way rather than in adorning his person; and besides, out of his forty pounds a year he was expected to keep a horse and droschky; for as chief judge of the town, his wife could not be supposed to go on foot when she went out for an airing.

His wife dressed well, and in the afternoon always appeared in silks and satins, and moreover, had some rather handsome jewels.

The judge's house was fairly furnished, as upon all his own and his wife's name-days, any little articles that they might have dropped a hint they wanted to make their castle comfortable, would be surely presented by one or other of the town tradesmen, particularly by any of them who were of a litigious disposition.

Roman Romanovitch was a jolly fellow in his house, and could eat, and drink, and have his joke with every one; and no wonder, for his wine-cellar was much better stocked than the neighbouring "Barrin's," although the latter had a good estate of some twenty thousand acres, and the judge could always boast that he never owed anybody a copeck. Which was true in one way, because all his creditors lived in his own town, and in the case of a disputed account the judge could not be expected to commit such an absurdity as deciding against himself.

The Courts were held in the Government House, a large ugly pile of bricks and mortar, that had been stuccoed over at some early time, and which, with its windows tumbling out, its creaking, rickety staircase, and generally dirty and dilapidated appearance, looked more like a ruined factory than a court-house.

The Court itself was a moderate-sized room, containing a long table, with a greasy ink-stained cloth, stretched over it, and a few forms and chairs.

At the end of the table sat the judge, with his clerk by his side. What *he* was like may be pictured from the description of his master. In front of the great man was a raised wooden desk, always covered with a mass of papers; and arranged handy for Roman Romanovitch were the ponderous volumes containing those thirty thousand statutes of the old law, out of which he had no difficulty in extracting an authority which would allow him to settle the cases how he pleased. .

But the judge himself did not constitute the Court.

In the middle of the table a triangular gilt pedestal stood, upon the sides of which some words were written, and close by was a small gilt representation of the immortalized double-headed eagle. Upon the judge taking his seat, the eagle was popped on to the pedestal, the whole thing then looked like one of the gingerbread figures seen at a country fair.

This constituted the Court, and by some legal fiction difficult to understand, the Emperor was then supposed to be present.

So long as this eagle remained on his perch, no unseemly noise could be made. To swear was almost death. To laugh even was attended by the imposition of a heavy fine. Bad language was an imprisonable offence, and even smoking was prohibited.

But immediately the eagle had flown down

again to the table; in spite of judge and clerk, smoking, talking, laughing, and swearing were all allowed.

To show the respect in which that royal bird was held, I came upon the judge once arranging his business in a back room; it was rather hot, and he had his coat off, but when he came into " open court," he had put it on.

In some of the cases which came before Roman Romanovitch, the parties interested would be represented by a lawyer or " advocate," as he is called in Russia.

This would be a nervous time for the judge, for then he could not manipulate those thirty thousand statutes as he used to do on the other occasions, and in the decisions which he gave then, he was obliged to have some little regard to common sense. Advocates were looked upon by Roman Romanovitch as his common enemies, and only established to rob him of his daily bread.

The decisions of the judge did not give universal satisfaction; but upon hinting to the townspeople the idea of a change, they thought that if he were superseded, they might very likely get a worse one, and so remained quiet.

Some of Roman Romanovitch's examinations of his witnesses were wonderful, for he was a stupid, ignorant dolt, and very often found himself checkmated in his cross-examinations, by one of the mujiks. For, although the rule of the law was that all the proceedings must be written, an oral examination by the judge was allowed.

By the time that the new law was introduced, and Roman Romanovitch necessarily relieved from his duties, he had amassed enough to live upon comfortably, and now exists bitterly bewailing the extravagance of a Government which pays its judges fair salaries, and as a consequence gets honest men.

Gospodin Ponomareff was the gentleman whom the town hailed with delight as the new dispenser of justice. He was a man of education, and without having any great experience in law, knew enough about it to give his decisions according to the new code, which is comparatively simple.

He was a gentleman, and even his clerk was a superior man to poor Roman Romanovitch.

At first the people hardly understood or comprehended the justice and the expedition with which cases were treated. In the jolly old paying days when justice was bought, a case would last for years, now weeks were sufficient.

Moreover, the new judge did not bully people, and the mujiks could not make out why they were not sworn at and cursed as they used to be.

The shopkeepers got paid for all they supplied to the judge, and, in consequence, for the first time since the Empire existed, the merchants competed for the custom of the judge.

The Court was a great improvement. A respectable room, with a portion railed off for the public, a proper witness-box, and a bench for the judge to sit upon, who dressed respectably, and with his chain and badge of office looked something like a judge.

The new administration of justice is entirely altered. Where evidence all used to be written, now all is oral: the accused stands face to face with his accuser, and *hears* what the witnesses swear to.

Our new judge had not half the power the

old one had; and in heavy cases the judgment of two or three such as I have described was necessary.

The new judge did not keep a carriage, and did not give so many dinners as his predecessor, although his salary was four thousand roubles, or five hundred pounds a year, against the other one's forty.

If this judge felt any difficulty in deciding a case, he remitted it to the Court above his, where the litigants had the advantage of a jury.

In fact, the administration of justice was turned topsy-turvy, and I think my readers will allow the superiority of the new over the old judge.

THE VILLAGE MUSICIAN.

CHAPTER XXIII.

BAZAARS.

IN common with other Eastern peoples, the Russians delight in bazaars.

Whether it be in town or country, your true Russian prefers to spend his money and lay in his supplies from the " Gostinoi Dvor " rather than from the open shop, or from the bazaar rather than from the merchant.

It is thus, that in the Gostinoi Dvor of a town the stranger will meet and observe every class of inhabitant. Whether prince or colonel, merchant or footman, servant or Pope, all will be seen jostling one another, and shouldering their way along: all engaged in one common object, endeavouring to get more than their money's worth for their money.

In large towns these bazaars are necessarily more extensive than in the smaller places, but with this exception they are much alike. Common covered-in buildings, with radiating alleys or streets, containing dark holes as shops, from which the merchants look out with vulture eyes on the passers-by, whom their touts on the threshold strive to persuade to enter as purchasers, whilst in a dismal sort of chant they describe the value and the goodness of the wares within.

For the convenience of both buyer and seller, different trades have different alleys, or " lines," as they are named, appropriated to them.

The shops or stalls, as most of them may be called, are with some exceptions very mean-looking; very little of the merchandise for sale is exposed to view, but the wealth of the contents of some of these places—jewellers for example— is enormous.

The bargaining which accompanies all sales is

a matter of much time and an immense amount of talk. It is a curious fact, that although the price of the goods may have been settled in their own minds by both buyer and seller, and although both sides are aware of the price so fixed, a bargain is impossible until double the amount has been demanded; after which, with very much chaffering and not a little swearing, the articles at last change hands for the sum of the intended ultimatum on both sides.

Naturally in these bazaars the shopkeeper or " merchant," as he is always described, is of the old-fashioned type. With his long beard, round close cap, long, ungraceful-looking coat, and high leathern boots, Ivan forms a good foreground to his shop, as sitting on a small wooden chair, balancing on the tip of his fingers the saucer containing his glass of tea, he is whiling away the time before closing, engaged in playing a game of draughts with his neighbour.

In these congregations of genuine Russians the " samovar " * is always heated, and it is one

----

* Tea-urn.

continual " brew " of tea all day long. All large bargains are concluded at the " traktir," over innumerable glasses of this steaming and fragrant beverage.

These real, old-fashioned traders, these hereditary merchants of the old school, men who have held fast to the traditions of their ancestors, who have not aped the frivolities and extravagances of the modern merchant, who still keep simple homes of their own, and who bring up their families honestly and respectably, are useful pious people; they neglect no Church ordinances, and strictly observe every holy day and fast day. They are, moreover, very economical in their habits, as one may easily prove on the spot. If you observe the man who has the tea in his hand, you will see him help himself to the smallest lump of sugar he can find. This he will not put into his glass; no! that would be far too extravagant, but he will bite a small piece off one corner, and putting this atom between his teeth will draw the tea into his mouth over it, so by this means his one lump of sugar will last almost the whole samovar out.

The alleys have several gaudy pictures of saints hanging about them; every act of a Russian's life would be incomplete, and unlucky, unless carried on under the protection of his patron saint. Several neighbours club together the necessary funds to keep the lamp before the picture constantly burning, and thus they believe their belongings to be more secure in their absence than they would be without this holy protection.

In these places all people go for actual business, and it is not at all an unusual occurrence, upon entering one of these stalls, for the proprietor to say, " We are very busy now, we cannot possibly attend to you, will you be pleased to call again."

Here, then, in short, is collected together every imaginable description of merchandise, amongst all sorts and classes of people; everything can be bought, from a paper of pins to a diamond necklace, from a pound of beeswax to a Paris-made umbrella.

These assemblies of commercial stalls, for they are nothing else, are extremely useful in a country

A VILLAGE BAZAAR.

To face p. 172.

like Russia, from the advantage they possess that when once under their roof, the buyer can supply all his wants without having to wander in the streets from shop to shop, either fainting from the intense heat of the sun, or at other seasons wading through a sea of mud which no boots can stand with impunity.

One great feature to be noticed in these city bazaars, is the number of money-changers in proportion to the other dealers. These men deal largely in silver coins, principally dollars, which, so far as I can find out, make their way in time through Siberia to China.

A few of these changers are Armenians, a few more members of the " old faith," but the majority are of that extraordinary sect called Scoptsi.

The principal portion of the money-changing business of Russia is in the hands of these Scoptsi, who, in this respect, may be said to occupy the place of the Jews in Western Europe.

The organization of the sect is peculiar, particularly as regards their wealth, which appears to be placed in a common fund, and managed by their priests.

A few years ago a small tribe of this fraternity were pounced upon in Moorschansk, a town in the Government of Tambov, and the accumulated treasures of years, in the shape of some millions of roubles, went partly to benefit the Government, but principally the police.

The tenets of this association are too disgusting to chronicle; and it is sad to be obliged to add, that in spite of the endeavours of the Government to crush this fungus of society, the members daily increase, though the punishment awarded to the brethren when discovered is deportation to Siberia.

A few years ago this sect found many recruits from amongst the soldiers; these were in their turn all transported to Maram, in the Caucasus.

Among other singular beliefs, exceedingly difficult to discover, in consequence of the jealousy with which all their secrets are guarded, these Scoptsi acknowledge a living Saviour, as well as a living Virgin, the difference of their belief in the two being, as far as I can understand, that whereas their Saviour exists for his life, their Virgin is changed yearly. Always chosen as a girl, she is first bought from her parents, and then admitted into the sect with cruel ceremonies.

In spite of what has been written concerning the " Sects " of Russia, very little is known about them, and the study of the question would be a profitable and interesting work for any one.

After this little digression, to return to the bazaars. Those of the country places are very different to the town Gostinoi Dvors; they are held sometimes twice a week, and, excepting a few fixed sheds arranged in " rows," the greater part of the merchandise is exposed for sale in the open air. They are generally held on the land belonging to the " Barrin," and in consequence a tax is levied by him on every person vending commodities on his ground.

All who can, within a radius of many miles, will flock to these fairs. The gentleman comes more to chat with his friends than to buy; the Crown official invents an excuse in order to enjoy the little distraction to be met with; the doctor from the neighbouring town, anticipating the good dinner that is sure to be going on in the "Gospotsky Dom," or gentleman's house, finds that a patient calls him to this very spot. So, in fact, every one of any consideration manages to make his way there.

The mujiks come in shoals—some to sell, some to buy, others again, merely to gossip; and the day on which a grand bazaar is held is a general holiday. Sunday is a very usual day for this purpose.

The sight is a pretty one; all are well dressed in their best attire. The bright and varied colours give a singularly gay appearance to the crowd, and form a pleasant contrast to the sand of the surrounding steppes and the grimness of the wooden boxes called houses.

All kinds of merchandise are exposed for sale, and the same arrangement of classification is to be observed as in the towns.

Furs of every kind—bear, fox, beaver, wolf, and sheep skins are there in quantities. Many Tartar merchants are walking about, looking as sharp as needles, in their embroidered skull-caps, supplying the faithful with mosque slippers. Others of the same race are making large bargains in tallow; a peculiar feature of all large transactions being that hand-money will be passed over to bind the bargain.

Any quantity of wooden articles, such as bowls, spoons, bottles, and tubs, of all sorts, colours, and varieties, betraying their Eastern pattern, can be purchased.

Salt fish is a large article of trade, owing to the numberless fasts, upon which, for the orthodox, this is the staple food.

Millet-seed and buckwheat are bought largely, principally by the better classes, these being a favourite dainty at their meals.

Harness and sledges; carts and horses; pottery and saints; linens and cottons; bristles and lard; caps and boots; champagne and English beer; truffles and wax candles; cigars and velvet; lace and French gloves; silks and satins—in fact, everything is sold here.

There is plenty of vodka-drinking, a great deal of talking, much discussion of neighbouring affairs, but no rioting or unseemly row, and it is a rare circumstance indeed to see the "sotsky," or village policeman, taking anybody to the lock-up.

At these bazaars all are assembled for business and gossip. No amusements are provided, and there is even no music.

Some few of the frequenters have come long journeys, as the mujik is beginning to find out that he can sell his productions at a more remunerative rate to himself by carrying them to the place of consumption than by disposing of them to the small merchants in his own village.

Occasionally foreign dealers penetrate into the interior; and in the very centre of the empire I have seen a dealer, who himself, cart, horse, and wares, were all Teutonic, and had wandered into these distant regions from the centre of Germany. I don't think, poor fellow, his success would warrant many more of his countrymen following in his steps, as immediately the mujiks found out he was a German, they refused to deal with him. Nothing or nobody do the mujiks hate so thoroughly as a German.

They have not yet forgotten the fact that, when they were still serfs, it was the people of that nationality who, as stewards or intendants of almost all the large estates, ground their very life's blood out of them in the shape of extra work and increased taxes. This feeling, quite rabid amongst some of the peasants, will exercise a great effect should at any time the Teutonic be arrayed against the Russian race in war.

It is at these country bazaars that the large amount of forged notes made in the empire get circulated. This business is a regular trade; there are established dealers in the article, and as these ply their avocations pretty openly, it would not appear very difficult to put a stop to this roguery were the police a little sharper.

By far the largest of these country bazaars are those of Nijny Novgorod, held in the month of August, where the turn-over last year amounted to nearly twenty millions of pounds sterling, and which was frequented by upwards of 250,000 people. That of Irbit, in Siberia, which takes place in February, is only second in importance, and there the interchange of commodities is also immense. Quantities of goods are sent to this place from Central Asia, although Irbit is much out of the direct route. A large trade is done in cottons, silks, and shawls, dried fruits and precious stones, all of which are brought from Bokhara and Khiva. Tea comes overland, viâ Kiatka. Furs of the most *recherché* description, sable skins, nearly black, are an important article at this market. In fact, a general assortment of almost all articles of necessity and luxury is offered here to the wealthy Siberians.

A prominent characteristic feature, and a bad one, of this February gathering, is the card-playing, not mildly carried on for amusement, but gambling in all its hideousness.

Not only do many Jews find their way from the innermost parts of Poland, perhaps requiring four weeks' time to make the journey, but black-legs and swindlers from all quarters assemble, together with broken-down Tchinovniks, dis-carded officers, and ruined aristocrats, who are all attracted by the scent of roubles, to try their luck in this hotbed of plunder.

The illicit dealing in gold also goes on in this place.

The Russian Government does not allow gold to be purchased by any one but themselves; and besides only giving a fixed price for it, according to assay, deduct a tax of fifteen per cent. from the fortunate diggers. This monopoly is guarded with great jealousy, and to such an extent that in the town of Ekaterienburg, on the frontiers of Asia, where the mint exists to which all gold must be brought from that part of the empire, *no worker in the precious metal is allowed to carry on his trade.*

The gold stolen from the Government washings and other places must, of course, be disposed of in some way; and it is to Irbit that it is all sent. There the natives from Khiva and Bokhara are the principal purchasers. The Jews are also said to convey annually a good round sum with them on their return to Western Europe.

The importance of these bazaars is gradually dying away. Before the introduction of railways they were absolute necessities; the people depended upon them for their supplies, both wholesale and retail, and so this Asiatic manner of doing business continued.

The increased facilities for locomotion of the present day is changing all this; and before long another of the bygones of Russia will be its provincial bazaars.

CHAPTER XXIV.

THE Russian traktir has been mixed up in the minds of most people with the kabak or vodka-shop; this is a slight mistake.

Every village of any size has its traktir or eating and drinking-house, the liquor supplied being vodka, mead, beer, and tea; for this latter beverage, since their emancipation, is drunk by the mujiks. The samovar, although a national institution, was not formerly much used by the mujiks in country villages; and I have often met people of both sexes who did not know the taste of tea.

In the traktir, the peasants make their bargains, the " foreign " merchants stay there on their annual trips through the country, collecting the goods which they have in many instances bought and paid for the year before. The affairs of the commune are discussed. Those little " plants " and " dodges " which the mujiks delight in are there arranged. It is where the local Tchinovniks are taken and feasted, and, in fact, answers to our country inn.

The vodka-shop is quite a different place, and it is this that is the curse of a Russian village. Very often a miserable shanty, with scarcely a roof over it to protect the drinkers from the weather, hidden away in some remote dark part of the village, and kept by one of the worst characters in the place; nothing is to be seen in the interior in the shape of furniture, but a table and couple of wooden benches. A few carboys of vodka on the floor, and half a dozen of small glass tumblers rolling about on the table, are the only signs of refreshment.

When a mujik drinks, he does so on a curious

principle, he does not do so for company's sake or in order to have a chat over his grog, but simply to get drunk. This is the only possible manner to account for those instances where a really good sober workman is always to be found drunk on his great holiday, say at Easter time. For months and months beforehand such a man will weekly lay by a few copecks in order to have his regular break-out at Easter.

A man on entering such a place calculates his means, and orders accordingly glass after glass as far as his money goes. The contents of these he bolts as quickly as he can, and as a rule, only a few moments will elapse before his head is on the table.

He is allowed to snore for a short time, and according as fresh candidates present themselves for a seat, the insensible brother is helped to the door, and with a good push in the middle of the back, launched out into the street, so as not to fall down on the immediate threshold.

The lumps of insensible humanity lying outside such a shop in the nights of Easter week are a curious spectacle to behold ; and as the wives arrive to find their missing husbands, a good deal of sorting has to take place before the right Ivan is found.

Some curious sights are at times to be seen in these dens: the people are such a singular mixture of honesty and dishonesty. I have seen a man who having paid beforehand for five glasses of spirit, was knocked over at the fourth, and then actually held up with one arm by the keeper of the place, whilst the glass was held to the lips of the unconscious customer, whose still thirsty gullet swallowed the contents.

These places are the source of the majority of the crime in rural Russia. A strict law exists against the keepers of vodka-shops taking articles in pawn, but actually they are the receivers of all the stolen property in the neighbourhood. Never mind what the article brought, it must be of very small value, indeed, if not worth a glass of vodka.

A fact for observation is, that a row is never seen in such places. A mujik when drunk is not quarrelsome. His intoxication generally takes an amatory form; and when they are drunk is

the time to see the mujiks embracing one
another.

Any great improvement in the social position
of the mujik must be preceded by a better supervision of the drinking-shops.

I once saw a case of detective business carried
out in reference to a kabak, which I think might
do credit to our English force.

The originator of the idea was a warehouse-
keeper at one of our mining stores, where he
found the candles served out to the miners were
used up much quicker than they ought to be, and
he was quite certain they were sold for drink at
the vodka-shop. The keeper of the place denied
it ; and the warehouseman proceeded in the
following manner.

He brought some candles into the office, and
there, in the presence of witnesses, inserted some
small pins in the candles in a particular manner.
The candles in time were served out to the
miners, and a few days afterwards a descent was
made on the kabak, the keeper of which still
swore he had received no candles, when the warehouseman taking up the lighted candle from off

the table, said, " Ah ; but who put these pins in ? "
and after examining them added, " Why, I did, to
be sure."

The consumption of candles fell off rapidly,
immediately this discovery was made.

BLACKCOCK SHOOTING.

CHAPTER XXV.

BLACKCOCK SHOOTING.

"IT is twelve o'clock, Barrin, and time to start," said my head forester, entering my cabinet one night in the month of April, for I intended to have a morning's blackcock shooting.

"All right, Vassily, see to the guns and provender, and we'll be off."

It was a fine moonlight night when I got into the tarantass, and we bowled along as fast as three horses could take us, for we had many versts to cover before the first break of dawn.

After once leaving the village, our road lay entirely through the forest ; and what a charming scene a forest presents when seen by moonlight. As we dashed through, just catching glimpses of the strange forms which the trees appear to take in the beautiful light and shade thrown on them, now and again hearing the bark of the still hungry wolf hastening to his lair from his depredations on the plain, I listened to my forester, as he was, as usual, enlightening me on the mysteries of the village commune.

By-and-by we saw a small fire ahead of us, and knew that to be the rendezvous where some of our under-foresters were waiting with horses in order to penetrate into the wood.

On arriving at this spot, we found we should be a little too early on our ground, and so elected to wait by the fire for a time in preference to doing so in the wood. Covered up in our sheepskins, we lay on the ground, and after half an hour's snooze started for the place.

It was a considerable clearing, some distance in the forest, that all the cocks in the neighbourhood had chosen for their fighting-ground, it being the habit of this bird, when once it has chosen its battle-field, to keep to the same for that season.

Upon arrival at the place, we separated into three parties, myself and an under-forester going to a spot indicated, where I found a small hut made of young pine-trees, so arranged as to look as nearly as possible like a natural clump. My man having stuck up a few stuffed grey hens in the neighbouring small birch-trees, we entered our hide, shutting the leafy door after us. I first of all made some small holes in the sides of the hut, in order to see clearly and to fire through, and then, as it was still dark (the moon having gone down), I sat down, lighted a cigar, and waited for the birds to appear.

While it was yet dark, so that I could see nothing distinctly, I heard a noise which was so loud that I imagined it to be the head forester operating on his "call," as he was very cunning at "calling" all sorts of game-birds. To my astonishment, the mujik with me commenced crossing himself, which at once showed me that the game had arrived. He also began in a most excited manner to point about, and intimate that

I should shoot (speaking was prohibited). I looked out, and certainly saw some things come flashing by, exactly as we see owls in the evening, but could not distinguish what they were; and as there is a game law in Russia which prohibits any one to kill hens during this season, I did not care about shooting. I could also just discern plenty of pot-shots up in the trees, but altogether the birds were so numerous, that I was fairly bewildered with the noise they made.

In a few minutes day began to dawn, and then I saw a really pretty sight, as the cocks, with the reddest of combs, and their tails displayed, were fighting one another like real warriors; whilst the hens were contemplating their mates with delight from the trees.

The quantity of birds that came to that spot was remarkable. I kept firing as fast as ever I could load, and the reports from the two other hides on the same ground were as continuous. The cocks hardly noticed the reports from the guns; perhaps would fly up for a moment, but only to return immediately, whilst the hens remained so disgracefully nonchalant in the trees that I was obliged, all laws notwithstanding, to make a clean sweep of them also.

I fired until my gun got almost red-hot, and was obliged to stop, when, as the sun just began to show its face, the birds all began to fly back into the high wood; the crowing and calling became more distant, and by the time the sun could be fully seen, not one single bird remained; the place was as quiet and desolate as when we first arrived.

We then crawled out of our hides and collected the spoil, which was sufficiently numerous to satisfy the most exacting sportsman.

In a few days' time we returned to the spot; and, in fact, all the time the pairing season lasts, say a month, one can shoot out of the same hides three times a week without scaring the birds away from their ground.

CHAPTER XXVI.

A CORPORATION DINNER.

THE invitation to which came about as follows:—

I once lived near a small town in the Government of Vladimir, of some fifteen thousand inhabitants, a place nevertheless famous for trade.

A telegraph to connect the town with the nearest station, some eighty miles distant, was much wanted by the inhabitants; but they were mean, and would not pay for it.

A subscription was proposed, but with no response; and no wonder, when I relate that the enterprising mayor, anxious to give his fellow-citizens the means of obtaining good water, had a short time before this built water-works, and erected supply-pipes and fountains at his own expense, presenting them all free to the town, and the response of the townspeople to this generous gift was: " It is all very well your giving us these water-works, but who is going to keep them in order; will you give us enough money for that purpose as well ? "

These people then, in common with all townspeople in Russia, were most abominably mean in paying for any description of improvement, so, as we wanted the telegraph very badly, the mayor and ourselves built the line between us, and presented it to the Government, who had agreed to work it. The advent of the telegraph in the town was, of course, a great event, particularly as it had not cost the people a copeck, and, therefore, a dinner was given to the founders of it.

The entertainment commenced with "sakuska," or what I call ante-dinner. This is partaken of standing, from side-tables, and upon this occasion consisted of caviare, cheese of many varieties, salted herrings, smoked salmon, radishes, sardines, anchovies, and numerous different sorts of dried fish, all of which are eaten with bread and butter.

The accompanying drinks were a caution. These were arranged on an adjoining table, bottles of every colour, form, and description,—all being labelled with gaudy *étiquettes*, as is the universal custom in Russia. There was cognac and sherry, gin and whisky, golden water and noyau, in fact, every wine, spirit and liqueur to be thought of. Little glasses were placed on a small tray, and in order to do justice to Russian hospitality, I had to take one of the small glasses in my hand, and, commencing with the first bottle, which happened to be white port, take a schnapps from each and every one in the order in which they stood, until I came to the last, which happened to be red port.

It was now time for the dinner to commence.

I was favoured with the seat of honour. As I have previously mentioned in this book, it is not the custom for the host to sit down with his guests, and on this occasion the mayor was running about the room all the dinner-time, now and again munching a mouthful at a side-table.

On my right and left were the marshal of the nobility as representing the people, and the chief judge as representing the Crown. The other tchinovniks were placed about in their proper order of precedence, and the merchants according to their position, as of the first or second " guild."

Most of these men were decorated with massive medals, suspended from the neck, principally rewards given by the Government to successful traders or inventors; and they take the place amongst the trading community of the different orders of knighthood.

All the company I have mentioned above were seated in one large room, which was separated by pillars only from another room and recess, in which the third " guilders," burghers and retailers were placed, and a very good thing the division was, as the sequel will show.

The dinner was good, including, of course, that dantiest of dainty fish, the sterlet, venison, bear hams (which when properly smoked are delicious), &c., and was, of course, served *à la Russe.*

The drinking was very furious, and in this class of society, when challenged to take a glass of wine, the glass must be filled to the brim, and the whole contents swallowed. A head of stone is required to keep itself steady, as the wine is mixed without any regard to its being sweet or sour, strong or light.

The Mayor, all the time most active in looking after the comfort of his guests, only arrived at the head of the table during the intervals between the courses of the dinner, to propose the toasts.

These were the Emperor, the Ministers, the Governor, and the principal guests, always presented to the attention of the visitors without anything like a speech, and drunk in champagne, the universal wine for drinking healths in Russia.

The toasts were received with wild acclamations in one room, but with thunders of applause from the smaller fry in the adjoining one; this explained, no doubt, the reason of their separation from us. A few of these visitors *did* get drunk, and as a favourite amusement of theirs was drinking the toasts standing up on a chair, with one leg on the table, the noise from time to time as one and another would lay himself down, falling amongst the glass and crockery, was something terrible.

All dinners must come to an end, and so at last did ours, with the usual finish of coffee, tea, and papirosses. And after that the third and noisy division were either turned out or dismissed, I could not make out which, and cards were proposed.

Surely it is a mistake to suppose cards were invented by the French for the amusement of King Charles. I think they must have a Slavonic origin, as a Russian of any standing in life loves his cards as much as he does his saint.

The principal game at cards played by the Russians is called "preference," which does not assimilate to any of our English games. Another one is called "Karolasch," which is our whist without trumps, whilst the gambling games are lansquenet, brag, &c.

The marshal and judge kindly proposed to

teach my English friend and myself Karolasch, which they did, losing a few roubles for the honour of having taught us, after which, getting into our sledge, we intended going home. The distance was forty miles only, but our unfortunate sledge-driver had also enjoyed the mayor's kind hospitality, and instead of driving home, lost his way, and when I woke up in the early day-dawn, found him driving us round and round in a large circle, a performance he had been repeating all night, so that instead of seeing our own church steeples, we were still in sight of those of the town.

This was the last time I saw that mayor, as he died shortly afterwards. Few men in Russia excelled him in common sense and shrewdness, and no man excelled him in the good he did for his native town, where the name of Yermakoff will ever be respected.

CHAPTER XXVII.

THE ARISTOCRACY.

THE old Russian aristocracy are not, I fear, an improving class; must be looked upon as a race now happily dying away from the scene, and will in time yield their place to that great middle class which is now springing up over the length and breadth of the empire, which is *the* one that will ultimately regenerate and raise up their country.

Any ordinary observer of the Russian people will come to this conclusion very readily.

In taking up and reading accounts of what the nobility were five-and-thirty years ago, I find them to be the same people they are to-day.

Their boys, perhaps, until fourteen years of age, invariably are under the dominion of governesses. Their education being confined to French, German, arithmetic, and dancing; on arriving at man's estate their knowledge of history or things in general is *nil*.

One never sees these people reading; or, if a volume is occasionally noticed about a house, it is sure to be the last production of Arsène Houssaye; and a Russian aristocrat can give a much better account of the last race for the Derby than he can of the life of Peter the Great.

At the same time I gladly admit their general politeness of manner; for their hospitality I know no people who can equal them; but, as far as I have been able to observe, as a class they have outlived their day, and nothing else can happen but their gradual decline and disappearance from the stage, as I have remarked above.

The real ignorance, or perhaps what may be described as the stupidity of these people, can hardly be conceived, as the following anecdote will prove.

The actor in it, since dead, poor fellow, a great

and kind friend of my own, well educated for a Russian, who had travelled abroad and seen the world, served many years in the Guards; was altogether, I believe, the best specimen of a Russian aristocrat I ever had the fortune to meet — a man withal who would do any kindness for another, and of whom it might be truly said, "that he was nobody's enemy but his own."

Like all of his class, he was very extravagant, and rarely had any funds in his possession, for, what with his military expenses, the cash he wasted upon his stud of horses, the taxes he was continually remitting to his peasants, his impecuniosity was proverbial.

He came to me quite joyfully one morning, announcing the receipt of a decent estate, together with a sum in money amounting to about two thousand-pounds, which some distant relative had been kind enough to leave him.

My friend was a great gourmand, and had a passion for shell-fish, and this was how he spent his legacy.

I went to town one day, and soon found out the prince was in his usual impecunious condition.

"Where has your legacy gone to?" I asked.

"Why," he replied, "you know that I am very fond of lobsters, and having a river on my estate in the Government of Saratov, I thought I would try and acclimatize that delicacy there, but unfortunately I have spent all the legacy in the attempt without succeeding. I quite forgot the water was not salt."

CHAPTER XXVIII.

THE TCHINOVNIK.

I HAVE described how the *old* judge made his income and spent it; but, after all, his aspirations were so moderate that the account of him will give very little idea of the real *town* Tchinovnik, and I must therefore describe one.

Vassily Vassilyvitch Ribkoff had by some means found his way into the department of Ways and Communications as assistant "writer." I do not think when he entered the service he could really write; but that was of no consequence, because his father was high up in the same service, and there were many of the juniors who would help the son for the hope of the favour of the parent. .

But Vassily, although uneducated, had a large amount of that natural intelligence and sharpness so common in the Russian character, and from his position at the lowest desk in the room, carefully observed all comers, noted their manners and their wants. He also became very intimate with the soldier who opened the door of the department, and no day passed without the man receiving his ten-copeck piece when he assisted our friend to his coat.

The department which had secured the services of Vassily was not one of those noted for either its practical, sensible, or honest way of doing business, and so the young man saw much that at first astonished him.

He was always at his post; whereas his fellow-clerks, excepting on those days when the minister himself was expected at the office, usually honoured the place with their presence for about two hours only.

In short, Vassily was wide awake, and soon became complete master of all the affairs in the department.

His promotion naturally followed, and in course

of time he passed from every table in the room and became "head tableman."

The man had made himself so useful to his superiors that they wished to advance him immediately, even as high as the direction of the department, but that did not suit him; "head tableman" was the stopping-point he had fixed upon, and having reached the goal of his ambition, he meant to profit by it.

His reasons were very simple. All papers that went through his office must pass this table, and before they were forwarded to the director or minister had to receive the signature of Vassily Vassilyvitch.

This post, then, had always been fixed upon by our friend as the most lucrative berth he could secure, and having come to an arrangement with his friend the soldier, who opened the door, referring to a fixed commission upon the business he introduced,* ("for in those days whenever you wanted anything done in a department you applied to the soldier who opened the door, and asked

---

* "Russia in 1870."

him to whom to go, whom to pay, and how much to pay ") Vassily commenced to make his "income."

The business went merrily; every one in the room was satisfied, as all participated in the plunder. Vassily knew far too much to keep it all to himself, and, moreover, being of a most good-natured disposition, I believe he took a pleasure in helping those fellow-clerks who were starving on the miserable allowance paid them by the Government.

Uniforms must be worn by all the Tchinovniks; but, excepting on those days when the minister was coming, Vassily and all the others who could afford the luxury of a second coat, always appeared in civil attire. On " Black Friday," when his excellency did honour the department with his presence, Vassily, in the seediest of uniforms and minus his heavy diamond ring, looked as humble and poverty-stricken a Tchinovnik as one could wish to see.

In the course of time Vassily managed the whole business of this great office; his superiors were fools, and allowed him to do everything; if they did put a spoke occasionally in his wheel, he checkmated them by tendering his resignation, which he knew they dared not accept.

Considering the work Ribkoff now had to do, his pay was not very large,—some hundred and forty founds per annum, which I must, however, do him the justice to say, he did not draw, but left to be divided amongst his fellows.

His department was always busy, and money rolled into his pockets; he got more rapacious, and his demands became exorbitant. "Never mind," said the contractors, "we will stick the price on to the Government." And so they did; and the Government was most awfully swindled.

Vassily became extravagant; "easy come, easy go," was his motto; and "I want more money," was his daily cry to the Government contractors. And no wonder, when it is known that by this time, although the salary of Vassily was twelve hundred roubles a year, which he never drew, he had two fine lodgings, one in town, one in the country; he kept a couple of carriages for himself and another for his wife; his collection of pictures was unrivalled, the furniture in his

house was magnificent, his children were dressed
far better than those of the minister, and their
governesses and tutors were the first in their
profession. Vassily rarely showed his head out
of his own immediate circle. He had method in
his proceedings too, and often might be seen
haggling with a droschky-driver at the door of
the department, over the poor devil's fare of
a few copecks, and the mighty matter being
settled, he would jump in, drive to the corner
of the next street, where his own carriage was
waiting, then throw the isvostchik a rouble,
and smiling at the credulity of the Russian
public, drive away to a snug little dinner in a
villa on the islands.

Vassily seldom showed himself at the opéra or
ballet, the minor theatres secured his patronage;
he did not see so many of his superiors there,
and the company, particularly behind the scenes,
was more to his taste.

I never came near a man who could lie like
Ribkoff. He would tell his director that black
was white, and prove it to him, moreover, with
a *nonchalance* perfectly wonderful to behold; while

the director, who happened to be an honest man, although shaking in his shoes at the job he was about to condone, would sign the necessary papers like a lamb.

Vassily took all precautions to protect himself. One of his dodges was dealing in pictures, which every now and again he would sell for some fabulous sum to some imaginary person, so that when an occasional question was asked, " How is it that Gospodin Ribkoff can spend so much money ? Where does he get it from ?" " Oh, you know, he deals in pictures," was the reply.

Vassily Vassilyvitch enjoyed his position for some time, until his superior was changed, and replaced by a minister more able than his predecessor. Then Gospodin Ribkoff's resignation was accepted, and he retired from the ranks of the Tchinovniks with well-lined pockets, and the respect and admiration of the office.

CHAPTER XXIX.

A PROVINCIAL HOME.

"WHO are those women in the box yonder?" I said to my companion one night at the opera in Moscow.

" What, those with the yellow hair and painted faces?" he replied.

"Yes." "Why, they must be provincials— *French* merchants' wives."

The dresses of these ladies may be fancied from the little I have said above concerning them. Their toilettes on the whole were more suitable for the Alhambra than they would be for the French play.

The next morning my friend came to breakfast with me, bringing the information that the objects of my curiosity were the wives of two merchants, brothers, living in a town about two hundred miles from Moscow.

As we should have to pass through this very town in a few weeks, I thought I should like to make the acquaintance of these fashionables, to see how such people lived, so my friend, who knew everybody, obtained an introduction.

A few weeks after, we arrived at this town and made our call. The house was a fine one, as the merchants were well to do, and both brothers lived together. They neither of them had any family.

The arrangements of all Russian houses are very similar. A dining-room, destitute of furniture, with the exception of table, chairs, and buffet. A large saloon, with its grand piano, complement of chairs, two card-tables, couch, and small round table, leads to the drawing-room, of somewhat smaller dimensions, which contains the same amount of furniture, together with a few ornaments scattered about.

In this room, in front of each window, there is generally a marble pedestal supporting a clock, which faces the street, for the benefit, I suppose, of passers-by, but has a curious effect upon the visitor as he enters the room, and sees nothing but the works.

In good houses this room leads into the boudoir, arranged in much the same manner, but in a more costly style; and this again leads to the last in the suite, the bedchamber of the master and mistress. The front of this chamber is filled up something like a sitting-room, the beds being placed behind a screen, which separates it into two parts. The sleeping apartments of the other members of the family are packed away in any odd corners.

Now, in all the apartments I have described there is a noticeable want of comfort; few of those little knick-knacks so necessary for the polish of the room are to be seen. A few ugly petroleum lamps, pictures of. saints in the corners of every room, sometimes a vile daub or two on the walls, a few cigar-ash-holders, sconces for the candles, and a tawdry chandelier in the saloon, make up the ornaments of a Russian provincial house.

But to return to our ladies. They were at home and received us; but what a difference in their costumes! No chignons, no black eyebrows or rosy cheeks, no ribbons, jewels, or gloves; in point of fact, not two "baronnes," but very ordinary-looking, thick-lipped, yellow white-faced, fat women, with not a mark of intelligence about them, and, I am bound to add, remarkably dirty hands.

They were dressed in seedy loose dressing-gowns, which, when one of the sisters accidentally lifted it off the ground, displayed a down-at-heel slipper, and not the cleanest stocking.

In this particular house, as in most others, there was not a single book of any sort or description to be seen, but there were plenty of newspapers lying about.

We drank the everlasting tea, and the ladies joined us in smoking papirosses. We talked small talk, and took our leave. But the whole concern was dirty; the ladies were dirty, the tea-

glasses were dirty, the house was dirty, the
servants were dirty; and, no wonder, for, as we
afterwards found out, the ladies were aristocrats
by birth.

In the afternoon we received an invitation from
the husbands to dine, which we accepted by presenting ourselves at the appointed hour, viz.,
five o'clock.

What a change had come over everything.
The servant who opened the door was a swell,
the rooms glittered with wax candles, carpets
were strewed about on the parquet floor, the
flower-stands were full: it was quite another
scene. But what shall I say of the ladies, in
all the magnificence of their newly-purchased
Moscow fashions? There were the yellow chignons again, the blackened eyebrows, and the
roses had returned to their cheeks. The dresses,
what there was of them besides their trains (for
they were very *decolleté*), were magnificent, and
a jeweller would have envied the diamonds and
emeralds which these two beauties had hung
themselves in; their hands, moreover, were
washed, and the gloves were all that could be

desired. The get-up was first-rate, but the style abominable.

We were presented to the husbands, who were what are called *French* merchants, that is to say, had discarded the beard, the round cap, and the high leather boots, and appeared close-shaved in a suit of the fashionable cut. Wealthy men, leviathans in their own trade, they aped what they could not reach.

A local magnate or two made up the party, but no strange ladies. Russian ladies of this class like to monopolize the men.

The dinner was, of course, luxurious, the table well appointed, our welcome most hospitable. The habits of the people were not very polished, for the ladies tried to eat gravy with their knives, and a sharp observer might occasionally have noticed their forks appear much too close to their teeth for another purpose than that of eating.

The men talked shop, the women prattled scandal, dress, and the newspapers; there was nothing healthy about the conversation.

We inquired their pursuits. Did they play the piano? No. Did they sing? A little. What books did they read? Not many; sometimes a volume of Paul de Kock. Did they go out much? Very little, the roads were so bad. Did they have many visitors? Not a great many; when they did come they had nothing to talk about but dress and scandal. Did they go to church? Regularly, and fasted as well. But their great enjoyments were the *bals masqués*, where they could have some real fun, and their trip to Moscow, where they could see the world. At home there was not much more to do than play cards and sleep.

The dinner over, we lighted our papiross; but this time the ladies could not be prevailed on to smoke "in company," as they called it.

Uusually after a Russian dinner everybody goes away at once, the host and hostess probably having another engagement; but on this evening we stayed to play cards, the ladies being as avaricious and sharp at the game as the men.

The whole evening seemed to be one continual handing round of sweetmeats, cakes, and spirits, &c.

These ladies, it appeared, were the daughters of a poor aristocrat, and married these two merchants in order to get a good home; and they declared the chignons, the paint, and the toilettes were only used to please their lords and masters, who thought they were the correct thing.

My opinion, however, is, that this love of dress, show, and frivolity is inherent in the Russian aristocracy.

PEASANT INTERIOR.

CHAPTER XXX.

ON THE ROAD.

WHAT is a Russian road?   A broad, desolate strip of the field or steppe through which it passes; separated, sometimes by a little ditch, and always in Central Russia by what the mujik calls the " Boulēvard," from the land alongside.

Necessarily this public thoroughfare is very wide, as one-half of it must lie fallow, whilst the other is being used.   If it were not for this arrangement, the wandering peasant or the hard-working carrier, might be more frequently lost in the mud, than he is at present.

Full of bogs, and quagmires, and with the bridges tumbling down,—a journey by road in the central provinces of the Empire in spring and autumn is a sorry undertaking.

Shaken about in a tarantass, a conveyance like a large canoe or " dug-out," supported on its wheels by some half-dozen pliant poles,—the traveller sees little around him but perpetual forest or perpetual waste. The country is dreary, an occasional telegraph post, or a solitary birch-tree, are all the companions the passer-by will have on his route.

No nicely trimmed hedges, no pretty homesteads, no charming honeysuckle-covered cottages, must the traveller expect to pass on a Russian road. Nothing but staringly ugly wooden boxes, most painfully destitute of colour or picturesqueness, will he have to look upon. All is ugliness, gauntness, and sadness.

The roads are so bad in those parts, that the driver always sits sideways on his perch, with his legs hanging outside the telega in order to slip off comfortably when he comes to a hole larger than usual.

Even on the roads the love of the Russian for precedents is seen, as the man will never drive in a straight line, but always follows the rut as it winds along its serpentine course.

When the yamschik sings as he bowls along, the refrain is so melancholy that it only adds to the general sadness of the whole undertaking, whilst the caravans of carts passed on the road as they transport the merchandise from one end of the country to the other, are all so painfully alike that they hardly destroy the monotony of the way.

If the horses bolt, as they sometimes do, owing to a very common custom of the bit being put outside instead of inside the mouth, the jolting and bumping is so terrific that the little excitement is more than counterbalanced.

The very poorness of the land distresses one, and the patient mujik, as seen on the field literally only scratching up the ground with his wooden-plough, causes a feeling of sadness difficult to shake off.

Again, the traveller never can calculate when he will arrive at the end of his journey. Sometimes he can cover a hundred and fifty versts in the day, sometimes not twenty. On several occasions I have had to have the tarantass bodily lifted out of a hole, and more than once have sank almost out of sight in the morass. It is not at all an unusual occurrence to find the driver turning out of what he calls the " high road," and galloping across the field itself, and to be told in answer to the query, Why the man is making such a détour, that the bog a little further on the road is impassable.

Once upon nearing a town as yet some two versts off, I noticed a sentinel placed on the road, who stopped us. I demanded, " What is the matter ? " " Oh ! you cannot get into the town this way," replied the man, " the road is not safe." " Why not ? " I asked. " Only that yesterday morning we sent the post off from the town, in a tarantass and four horses, and we have lost the lot; tarantass, horses, mails, coachman and postillion have all disappeared in the bog," and he added, " Yes, it is a very bad road." And so I thought.

We were obliged to strike into the fields and absolutely to go a round of thirty versts, before we got into the town, the houses and churches of which seemed to be quite near all the time.

The only accommodation on the road is to be found at the post-houses, where one stops every twenty versts or so to change horses. The comforts in these places are of the very smallest possible description. A whitewashed room, a couple of chairs and a table, and a wooden sofa, are all the necessaries provided, whilst for luxuries a samovar with sometimes a glass or two to drink one's tea out of, are all the traveller must expect to find for a certainty.

Against all these drawbacks, one advantage is brought vividly to the mind of every traveller, that is, the safety to persons and chattels. I believe that a child could travel by itself all over Russia without any harm coming to it, whilst a foreigner, unable to speak the language, can travel into the innermost recesses of the Empire without being cheated. The mujik religiously believes that he must not cheat a fool, and as those who are unable to answer what he says to them are considered by him to be silly, he never takes advantage of their ignorance.

In all my travelling experiences in Russia I do not think I had to show my revolver twice, and on the only occasion that, to my knowledge, the use of a weapon was necessary, the incident was sufficiently curious to be worth quoting.

In the Government of Vladimir, on rather a quiet road, a report had got about that a traveller was carrying a large sum of money with him. This came to that traveller's ears, and although it was not true, he, thinking discretion was the better part of valour, purchased a pistol in the town, having left his own at home.

As he left the town that night, and was drawing near to the forest, the yamschik turned round and playfully asked him, "Ah! Excellency, what is that you have got in your belt?" "Only a toy," replied the traveller. "Will you sell it to me?" said the mujik. "It cost too much money for you to buy: I gave twenty-five roubles for it," answered the gentleman. "I'll give you that with pleasure," the man replied. "But what will you do with it?" "Keep it as a remembrance of the Englishman," responded this very interesting travelling companion.

The gentleman then requested the yamschik to hand him the tall steeple-crowned hat he was wearing, and pulling out his revolver, fired off a barrel, sending the ball in at one side and out at the other of the hat, and then addressed the man as follows:—

"You see the hole this toy has made through your hat—I have got five more of the same toys left; and if I see you speak to a soul on the road or pull up for an instant, I will send the whole five through your head in the same manner I have one through your hat. I have heard of your little game, and know what you are about."

The hint was quite enough; nothing was seen of the man's companions, although they were known to be on the road.

CHAPTER XXXI.

RAILWAYS.

THE year 1860 saw the vast dominions of the Emperor of Russia very sparely supplied with those necessary means of locomotion—railways.

Up to that year, with all its efforts, the Government had only been able to complete some six hundred and fifty miles of iron roads. Since then, however, the lost time has been made up, and now, though only eleven years have passed, Russia can boast that she has the very respectable distance of nearly ten thousand miles covered by railways.

The accommodation for travelling upon some of the lines is very perfect; for instance, on the line between St. Petersburg and Moscow, the traveller finds himself in a luxurious saloon, provided with the means for whiling away the time most comfortably. A game of whist, dominoes, draughts, or chess is at his disposal whilst the wax candles in scones on the sides of the carriage, together with the clock and other little etceteras, cause him almost to forget that he is on " the road." The comfortable bed in which he passes the night, the washing-stand with its good supply of water, are also vastly superior to the accommodation to be found even to-day in many of the provincial hotels.

The fares are not high; twenty-one roubles, or two pounds fifteen, cannot be considered an extravagant charge for travelling, with all the comforts I have enumerated, for a distance of four hundred miles.

The buffets and arrangements for refreshments are, on the whole, far in advance of anything we have in England.

Necessarily, the Russians have much to learn

in the management of their railways; the pace is slow, and much time is lost in the continual stoppages. At almost every station the Russian traveller requires, at the very least, to refresh himself with a glass of tea.

This mode of conveyance is, of course, vastly more rapid than the old tarantass and kibitka, so that the natives do not think anything of wasting a little time in " catching " the train at a country station. The mujik will frequently arrive at four o'clock in the afternoon for a train that is going to leave, say the next day at eleven; and if the traveller, in order to catch a corresponding train, should have to wait some few hours at such a station, he will see as much mujik life as will satisfy him for some time to come.

It is possible to go to all the principal points in Russia by railway: St. Petersburg is connected with Odessa, Moscow with the Sea of Azov. Corn can now come direct from the Volga to the Baltic; an unbroken line connects the Asiatic mart of Nijny Novgorod with the Prussian frontier; and whereas it was formerly necessary to go round by St. Petersburg to get to Moscow, the ancient Muscovite capital can now be reached direct from Berlin.

In winter, travelling by railway has its drawbacks: it is not an uncommon thing for the engine to be found imbedded in the snow, and for the traveller to wake up in the morning and find himself in the same spot where he was when he went to sleep the night before, all the attempts of the mujiks to dig the train out of the drift in the night having been futile.

Comparatively speaking, very few trains run on the Russian railroads, so that accidents are not of frequent occurrence, and when they do take place, are generally caused by the break-down of a bridge or a part of the road, owing to the scamping way in which the work has been done.

The first of these railways was constructed by foreigners; now the majority of the contractors are Russian; whilst it seems a difficult thing for Russians themselves to manage the lines, hence the principal engineers and officers are foreigners.

The guard of the Russian train is a very important personage, and being considered by the mujiks, from the opportunity he has of knocking them about, as the greatest man on the line, apes a position to which he has no claim.

I saw a curious instance of this. A gentleman and myself were the only occupants of a carriage on the Moscow Nijny line. I had fallen asleep, and woke up hearing my fellow-passenger talking to himself and making a great noise. I asked him what was the matter, when he told me that he had, on awakening from his sleep, found the guard sitting by his side, and he added, "I asked the guard what he was doing? He had no business there," to which the man replied, "I am the guard, and shall travel where I like." I then told him that I did not allow guards to travel in the same carriage with me, and then he got impudent, and I had no alternative but to take him by the shoulders and put him in the cupboard at the end of the carriage, where he is now safely fastened in.

I did not much like the idea of travelling all night with the guard locked up, and so at the next station had the little affair brought before the station-master, and it ended by the guard not being allowed to proceed, as, unfortunately for him, the gentleman whom he had insulted was a vice-minister.

CHAPTER XXXII.

A RIVER TRIP.

THE rivers in Russia are not noted for their beauties. On the Oka, and also on the Kama, a view which is passable can occasionally be seen; but generally the time of the traveller is more taken up with contemplating the stickings on the sand-banks than the beauties of nature.

Russian steamboats are by no means to be despised. The arrangement of classes is exactly the reverse of our own; the second-class passengers being more numerous, have the stern cabin, whilst the forward cabin is fitted up for the first-class. The third-class travel on deck, the whole of the afterpart of the vessel being covered over for their accommodation.

We started on our journey under favourable auspices. The weather was fine. We heard from the steward that the larder was well stocked, and that the wine-cellar had been attended to.

No sooner was the warp cast off from the pier than every mujik crossed himself many times, no doubt appealing to the Saints for protection on his journey.

Steaming down the Oka, with nothing to look at better than sand and steppe, we reached one of the oldest towns in the Empire. As a convincing proof of its antiquity, a day or two before we arrived there a large stone had been found underneath the foundation of an ancient house, which again was under the foundations of an ancient church. This stone had some bowls chipped out of it, which were full of silver coins. These cash-boxes had covers of clay over them, which had excluded the air perfectly, so that the coins were quite clean and bright. They amounted in number to some thousands, and some dated as far back as the time of the Ruric dynasty. The pattern and device of these coins were beaten out on the money, and some speci-

ON THE "OKA."

mens of it may now be seen in the British Museum.

There we received an addition to our passengers, in the shape of the governor of a neighbouring province, who, in all the glory of his new rank, was making this his first tour of inspection ; but, like all people, he preferred enjoying a cruise on the river to jolting his bones in a tarantass.

He was a curious, consequential little fellow : a general with a very red nose, which in the province from whence he had come, obtained him the sobriquet of " Champagne Ivan."

Attended by all the local magnates, he blustered and bullied a good deal, and was not best pleased when he found he was on what was called the " English boat," instead of that of the Russian company. Our boat was also owned by Russian peasants ; but as we had built it, it was con- sidered a foreign one, and his Excellency did not find himself so much sought after as he could wish. The local police officers accompanied him to the frontiers of their district, and, as they told me, were only too glad when they parted company with the great man, who felt it a necessary part of his duty to blow them up the whole route for real or imaginary want of supervision in the districts through which he passed.

Every now and again we touched a landing-place, always beset by mujiks, vending bread and such delicacies as liver, apples, &c., for the accommodation of our mujik passengers.

Besides the many quaint-looking Asiatic barges which, decorated as some were with many-coloured flags and curiously painted and carved trellis-work around their sterns, that passed us every now and then, sometimes singly, sometimes in numbers sufficient to form a little fleet, there was nothing but an occasional stray bird or two, and the common and constantly-recurring event of our touching the ground or fairly taking it, to distract us. Some of these light-draught built craft are of very large burden, carrying a thousand tons of merchandise, and have a regular wooden house erected in the centre of the deck for the accommodation of the crew.

The river abounds with shoals, which should have been dredged away, as a heavy tax is charged upon all merchandise floating on its waves. But the money, although paid, does not find its way out of the pockets of those who receive it, for any such purpose.

The pole was constantly in the hands of the mate, who, noting the depth from the painted marks upon it, cried out, " two and a half; two; two; one and a half," meaning one foot and a half. Our steamer could not have drawn more than eighteen inches of water when the usual bump occurred, and on we were—hard and fast. The whole crew then commenced to push the head of the boat round with long poles. The engines went full speed ; grate, grate, we heard the bottom stir up the sand, and we were in deep water again.

A mujik must always do everything he possibly can with gloves on his hands. Your common coachman is always gloved. Your gardener tends his plants with his hands carefully covered up, and the sailor or boatman has his enveloped in immense leather cases that impede his every movement.

We were just thinking what absurd things these gloves were for boatmen to wear, when the cry arose, " A man overboard !" The boat was stopped, a small skiff put off, but the poor fellow never rose again; he could swim, but his large boots and heavy gloves took him to the bottom like a stone.

This was an awkward accident for the captain, but a "paper" was immediately prepared showing the facts, and as we had a general governor on board who signed it, the captain felt secure from police interference.

We wondered how it was possible that with the slow manner of towing by horses, the barges, or "barks," as they are called, ever could reach their destination, some having already come, and some having yet to go, thousands of versts! As many as two hundred horses are sometimes only sufficient to drag these heavy lumbering things along.

By and by a hurricane arose. In a moment the whole scene was changed, the wind roared, and the waves leaped with tremendous fury. In a few seconds the boat was a-hull, exposed to all the power of wind and waves. Then we saw the captain in his proper character. He was amazed and scared, as it was the first time he had experienced such weather on the river, and having been a mechanic all his life, his knowledge of naval affairs in general was small.

He shouted his orders out indiscriminately: "Ease 'r!" "Stop her!" "Go a-head!" "Back her!" were all yelled out of the speaking-trumpet promiscuously; and the engineer, not knowing what he was required to do, did nothing, which sensible proceeding saved us from shipwreck, and allowed us to be blown on to the first sand-bank, where we stopped a minute or two till the storm lulled, and then went on our way rejoicing.

We had several Tartars on board, and as evening approached it was curious to watch them as they laid their tiny piece of carpet on the deck, and, kneeling on it, with their faces towards the setting sun, devoutly prayed to their prophet to protect their wanderings.

Here and there we got a glimpse of a pretty view as we approached the mouth of the river, and in time reached Nijny Novgorod, which, with its frowning Kremlin soaring above the town, could tell tales of glory, of days long since passed away.

As every one knows, the Oka discharges itself into the Volga, so, bidding our friends good-bye, not forgetting the great man, we took the ship's boat, and were rowed into the latter river, noticing on the way the wonderful diversity of the various merchandise with which the countless number of barges we passed were loaded.

We saw iron from Siberia, tea from China, cotton from Bokhara, carpets from Persia, petroleum from the Caucasus, salt from the Eastern steppes, corn from Podolia, herrings from Astrakan, samovars from Toula, grind-stones from the Oural mountains; in fact, a collection of articles, Eastern and Western, much too numerous to mention, for Nijny Novgorod is the point where, for transport purposes, Europe meets Asia.

We were soon at the steamboat which we hoped would carry us as far as Perm. This was not such a good boat as we had just parted company with, perhaps because there were no Englishmen to look after it. However, we got a comfortable cabin, and determined to enjoy ourselves, and, as we did not know the state of the larder, provided ourselves with a few delicacies.

The Volga resembles the Oka, with the exception of being much wider and more choked with sandbanks; but as our boat was much smaller we did not so frequently get aground.

We were a jolly party of three for this portion of the journey, and as we must do something to kill the time through the seven days that we should be on the route, we took to whist, and I think it was one hundred and eighty rubbers that we played on that memorable occasion.

The general sights on the Volga varied but little from those we had already passed through. Every now and again we passed a village. "Those ugly collections of grim timber boxes called houses, built entirely of wood, roofs and all, without a bit of thatch or patch of green, or a flower or spot of colour of any kind to enliven the sepia dulness of the place." The only showy buildings were the churches, invariably towering like venerable giants amongst the pigmy houses, which with their golden or variously-painted cupolas, were always saluted by the mujiks on board with many crosses on the face and chest.

An occasional town was seen, but nothing in

them seemed to offer any picture of novelty, and we soon came to Kazan.

This stronghold of the Tartars soon showed us we were nearing, if not Asia, certainly Asiatic manners and customs.

On the landing-place all the retailers were followers of the Prophet. The apples they dealt in were splendid. I know no apples to equal those grown in the south of Russia. They are very large, the flavour is good, and what is of great consequence in this fruit, a Crimean apple can be kept sound for a year.

These Tartars are beggars to deal with, and here one took me in beautifully. They deal in little barrels of grapes, which they sell per pound; but I noticed one barrel of a particularly nice description of fruit, and demanded, " How much a pound ?." " Cannot sell that barrel by the pound, as it is the only barrel of the sort here," replied this very gentlemanly-looking dealer. " How much for the barrel ? " " Three roubles," which was about the fair price, judging from what he was asking for the other sorts. " Is it full ? " I said. " Quite, "answered he; and began diving into the seed (all grapes are packed there in the husks of seed), and kept fishing up the grapes to show me the barrel was full.

As he would not sell it by the pound, I bought the barrel, and took it on board. The next day on emptying it, I found, instead of ten pounds, two: the man had fished up the same bunches, time after time, and done me. However, I consoled myself with the reflection that it might be worth my while once, for the sake of experience, to be " caught by a Tartar."

Before continuing our journey we went on board one of the boats just come from Astrakan. Amongst the passengers were a company of Bokharians, about seven in number, old and young. They were all very handsomely dressed, some more magnificently than others. There was one jolly-looking fat old man among them, who never moved without having in his arms, what I thought was a large brass water-jug. I put down the reason for his hugging this article, having to do with the Oriental custom of continually washing the hands. I made his acquaintance afterwards, and then learned that the old image was an ambassador from the Khan of Bokhara, to the Emperor, and that the brass water-jug was a golden water-bottle, a present from the Khan to the Czar; so no wonder the old man took care of it.

We now left the Volga, in its sluggish, creeping, yellow, muddy course to the Caspian Sea, and entered the Kama, which river we ascended. As yet we had been continually going down stream.

This river is not quite so wide as either the Volga or Oka, but the water is deeper, and there are not so many sand-banks. We got along quicker; but unfortunately, as the nights were dark, our captain would not go on all night, but stopped at the landing-place till day dawned.

When we got into the Kama, my friend the general, who was one of our party, came to me with the whisper, " Now, my boy, we *will* have some sterlet."

The Kama is renowned for the fine flavour of this, the greatest delicacy a Russian ever dreams about. So at every landing-place, never mind what time of day, early morning or dusk, the general carried me off to inspect the fish-stews.

At last, he came upon a fish about ten pounds weight, which we bought, and had cooked. It was delicious, but not large enough for the general, as the larger the fish is, the finer the flavour is supposed to be. After some more inspections we came on a monster of some twenty-eight pounds. Not only was this fish immediately secured, but the general insisted upon carrying it on board himself, for fear he should lose his expected treat.

The same evening this giant was cooked for the entertainment of the passengers in our part of the boat, who with the captain were invited to dinner. It was superb, and the old general, after the first mouthful, turned to me with " Bogo eto carasho ! " By G——, this is fine !

To enlighten the curious in such matters, I will say, that this fish cost us on the Kama eight roubles or twenty shillings ; it would have commanded in St. Petersburg, two hundred roubles or thirty pounds, and was supposed by the knowing ones in such matters to be at least one hundred years old.

We pass some pretty scenery. In a few places

it might even be called grand. The banks in many parts were of that Devonshire red colour, which amongst the grass and trees looks so pretty in the setting sunlight.

As in the evening, already very dark, we were feeling our way to the landing-place, we passed a solitary man on a raft. We noticed, first, the fire, which he had somehow rigged up on a pole, to warn steamers and barks of his whereabouts, and then saw him on his tiny raft of two or three timbers only, swiftly yet surely floating along the stream, upon which he was either being carried home to his village, or what is more probable, away from his imprisonment in Siberia, to some haven of refuge he hoped to reach.

So far as we had journeyed, some two thousand miles, we had observed no difference in the people, their houses, manners, or customs, excepting always the Tartars, whom I have mentioned. The salient points of the population are alike.

But we found very strong symptoms that we were getting further north and east,—snow appeared, ice came floating down the river. Occasionally we passed a fellow-steamer hurrying down empty, in order to escape being frozen in, whilst our captain began to fear he should not reach Perm.

It was not until the last day of our living on board the *Boyetz*, that we had fully brought before us where our journey was leading us to.

We came alongside a long, large sort of steam barge, the deck of which was covered over with thick iron wire, and on which were pacing a strong guard of solders.

Some standing staring idly at the waves, some sitting contemplating our freedom with looks of anything but happiness, others frowning with a fierceness which would seem to warn the guard not too suddenly to turn his back; all dressed alike in sombre clothes with yellow caps; we saw before us the last convoy of those unhappy wretches condemned to transportation to Siberia. Looking into the port-holes of the cabin prison below; shaved heads with maniacal faces, together with the clank of chains, showed us that we were looking on criminals so bad and so dangerous, as to need to be marked like this against any possibility of escape.

With this sight still in our eyes, we arrived at Perm, the present connecting link between Europe and Asia.

THE OURAL MOUNTAINS.

CHAPTER XXXIII.

THE OURAL MOUNTAINS.

THE Oural Mountains! What a distant place this sounds. What a bleak, cold, desolate idea the name strikes into our minds. It seems as though in passing them we should leave all civilization behind us, and see nothing the other side, but snow and ice, frost and bears.

What are the facts?

"Well, Ivan," we say, awakening from a most refreshing sleep, which the goodness of the road

from Perm to Ekaterienberg had allowed us to
have in our tarantass, " where are we ?"

" In the Oural," Ivan our coachman replied.

" Yes, all right ; but where are the mountains ?"

" Mountains !" he said, " why, here they are,"
pointing to some little hills we were amongst ;
and added he, " don't you see I have got a skid
on my tarantass, which is a proof we are among
the mountains !"

So, after all, the Oural Mountains are only
little hills in appearance, their real height*
being unnoticed by the traveller, owing to the
constant but gradual ascent of this, the last
road in Europe which he travels upon, so that
by the time he reaches the passes a great
portion of the altitude has been attained.

The scenery, however, is very pretty, although
not grand : hill and dale, wood and dell, water
and rock, offer at every point a charming peep,
and, besides, a good hard road with a sprinkling
of gravel on it, allows the traveller to be carried
along without being jolted to pieces, a luxury

---

* The greatest altitude is about 4,500 feet.

that few who have not travelled in Russia can properly appreciate.

The population *appears* to be large; but this is not the case. A traveller is induced to think so, perhaps, from the fact that in this part of the kingdom, the inhabitants generally locate themselves by the roadside.

Already we observe from the looks of the people, that we are approaching a more intelligent race of peasants than those we leave behind.

Every now and again the distant glare from the copper-smelting furnaces, and the dull thud —thud, of the hammer beating the iron into sheets, reminds us that we are in a centre of manufacturing industry.

The greater proportion of Tartars; the smaller number of churches; the appearance of the mosque with the quaint mollah from the little trap-door in the steeple calling the faithful to prayer, tell us that we are rapidly leaving European Russia behind us.

A crowd of gipsies of that singular dark type, with thick lips, straight noses, and long curling

jet black hair, veritable Egyptians in their appearance, warn us that we are on the road to Central
Asia, from which neighbourhood these people arc
continually wandering. These gipsies are not to
be confounded with those commonly met with in
the towns of Russia, from amongst whom the
singing and dancing bands are chosen, and who
are of a type similar to those which are found in
other parts of Europe.

The post-houses on this Oural road are generally
better than in the interior of Russia, and on the
whole we can jog along comfortably.

A little further on our way, in a quiet spot in
the middle of the pass, is an unpretending obelisk,[*]
with the ominous words Europe and Asia imprinted,
one on either side. Standing, then, with one foot
in Europe and the other in Asia, lighting the best
cigar we have with us, and opening our last bottle
of brandy, we drink success to that mighty empire,
whose dominion extends for thousands of miles to
east and to west of us, and whose limits may be

---

[*] Erected to commemorate the conquest of Siberia, by
Yermak the Cossack, in 1573.

said to show as yet no settled boundary towards the south, while only the polar ice confines it on the north.

Still going through the mountains, although descending instead of ascending, for we are now on the Asiatic slope, we see the same landscape that we have left in Europe; but just as the last field on the Russian frontier at Wirballen is always brown and barren, while its neighbour on the Prussian side of the little stream is at the same time green and verdant,—so here, immediately on our arrival in Siberia, all seems brighter and more intelligent compared to the ignorance and stolidity we have left in Russia.

In our journey through these pretty passes we have seen much to show us, that, besides the beauties of nature, riches also lie concealed beneath the earth. We have passed many works on the way, owning leviathan estates, from which they draw both the precious and useful minerals, some of them still industriously moving on, whilst others are left as monuments of the ignorance and extravagance of the Russian noble,—to be tenanted only by pigeons and doves.

As we enter a village in the middle of the
night we see a gaunt, half-clothed man, skulking
along in the shadow of the overhanging eaves of
the houses he is under. Approaching the windows,
he carefully feels to see if they are open, but feels
in vain : nothing daunted, he proceeds further and
further, from house to house, until he finds the
object of his search. Poor, hungry, half-starved
devil, with wild eagerness he feels inside the open
casement, clutches the lump of bread he finds on
the sill, hastily swallows the milk from the mug,
which he carefully replaces, then slinks back again
munching his crust, to the solitude of the forest
he has just left.

He is an escaped convict from Eastern Siberia,
and is walking his nocturnal way to some of the
large towns in Western Russia, in which he will
be safe from the observation of the police for a
short time. So, moving from town to town, he
will be a long time before he is discovered as a
man with no passport, and sent back as a prisoner
to the place he came from.

The Russian mujik has a tender heart towards
a fellow-creature in distress, no matter the cause ;

hence these kind souls place at their open window during the night bread and milk for these unfortunate wanderers to refresh themselves with.

As we drive up and down this hilly ridge,—northwards to the gigantic mountain of magnetic iron, christened by the original natives of Siberia "Blagodat," southwards, as far as to where the steppe commences to approach the southernmost spurs,—we are struck with the riches of this part of the Empire. Here are gold, copper, lead, iron in masses; forests in abundance, to supply the necessary fuel for the successful working of these minerals; labour sufficient for all purposes; all means and appliances ready at hand, the whole only waiting until a little more activity is instilled into the Russian character to be turned to account.

The gold question must one day exercise a great influence on the future of this Slavonic empire. Bearing in mind the extent of the auriferous country in Russia, the fact that no impediment of climate or labour exists to the working of it, and the low rates ruling for wages; also the (comparatively speaking) shallow depth at which

these immense riches lie, I am strongly of opinion
that when gold-digging is quite free and un-
trammelled with the fetters of the bureaucracy of
the Mining Department, the production of gold
in Russia will equal, if it do not rival, that of
Australia.

As I have before observed, the Oural Mountains
may be said to be the separating line of the ignorant
from the more intelligent portion of the Czar's
people. On the eastern side of the range the
peasants are more civilized and better educated
than in other parts of the Empire.

The political exiles who from time to time have
been sent from the centres of civilization to live
amongst them, having no business or employment to occupy them, passed away their weary
days in the laudable occupation of teaching the
peasants' children to read and write.

The people are also a finer race, and generally
better behaved; one of the most important proofs
of their superior intelligence being that the women
are treated much better by their men folk, and
hereabouts a woman is considered as something
else than a beast of burden.

The hospitality of these people is unbounded, and for travelling about there is no safer place in the world, as the following anecdote will prove :—

I happened to be enjoying the hospitality of the Government tutor of a large estate in the South Oural, when the merchant who had the contract for washing the gold on the estate, hearing I was going to the town of Ekaterienberg, offered to take me there, as he was about starting with his quarterly produce of gold.

I went to his house and saw the whole process of weighing and bottling this precious booty up in tin cases. Everything had to be done in order, and in the presence of his two partners, very intelligent mujiks, the head partner being a German.

The tin boxes were sealed up with many seals, several mysterious papers within being signed and countersigned ; the boxes then carried to the inner room, where the necessary eating before starting was about to commence.

We had a very jovial dinner, and at last it was time to start.

" Now we must arm ourselves," said our host.

" Arm ourselves ?" I replied. " What for ?"

"To conform to the regulations of the Government," replied the merchant; and producing a printed document, read from it certain instructions as to the arming of the gold escort with swords and pistols.

I had my revolver with me; my friend having left the room for the purpose, returned with a perfect battery of self-defence. An enormous horse-pistol, and two long German dirks, did he hang about his body. His two partners contented themselves with a pistol apiece.

The gold was placed in a tarantass, thrown in anyhow, and then, having, according to Russian custom, sat in a circle in perfect silence with all the family for a minute, and every one having swallowed a bumper of champagne, I mounted with the chief partner to keep the gold company, whilst his two friends preceded us in another tarantass.

We travelled for about fifty miles, and in the middle of the night arrived at a village in which one of my mujik acquaintances had a brother living, and nothing would satisfy our friend but we must go and see this brother.

We waited at the post-house whilst Nicolai Nicolaievitch went to see all prepared for our reception, and then proceeded to partake of his kind hospitality.

The horses were taken out of the tarantasses which were left in the open street, whilst we were enjoying a most comfortable supper. As is the custom, we must eat, and particularly drink, a good deal: during one of the few intervals when the bottle was not going round, I looked about me for the gold, and did not see it. Now I naturally felt morally responsible for those tin boxes, and got rather nervous at not seeing them.

Siding up to the German, I asked, "Where is the gold?"

"Oh! that is all right," he replied. "It is in the tarantass, outside in the street. It is quite as safe there as here."

Upon which answer I came to the conclusion that the dirks and pistols were a snare and a delusion, and that no much safer place could be found to travel in than the Oural Mountains.

CHAPTER XXXIV.

A SIBERIAN RESTAURANT.

IT was at the Hotel Post, kept by Mr. Plotnikoff, in the town of Ekaterienberg, that I first made the acquaintance of a Siberian restaurant.

The appearance of several chambers all handsomely fitted up with stuffed sofas and settees, well-curtained windows, together with the diningtables elegantly arranged with plate and glass, made me doubt whether I could really be on the Asiatic side of the Oural Mountains.

The bill of fare contained everything that any reasonable man could require, with the exception of sea-fish, this want being made up with an assortment of such fish as it was possible to bring up frozen to this distant place, such as beluga, sturgeon, accitrina—all very good eating, but, perhaps, a little too meaty.

For delicacies there were pâtés-de-foie gras, truffles, and all the other multitude of sauces, pickles, and condiments which one expects to find in a first-class restaurant in Western Europe.

The wines were of all sorts and descriptions, and not outrageously dear, as might have been supposed.

It is customary in all these places to have a band of singers, accompanied by a musician or two, who sing and play at intervals during the day, and nearly all night; they are lodged and fed by the proprietor, and "make what they can" out of the customers.

These musicians, like almost all the other money-making people in Russia, are Germans.

In such retaurants the people are very fond of making what they call "pic-nics." A dozen men sit round a table, and each one orders a bottle of wine or spirits; all are brought up at the same time, and the whole party drink round until the lot is finished. This mixing is not agreeable; perhaps it commences with port; brandy following, and champagne for a finish.

English porter is considered a very aristocratic drink, and is very often taken with powdered sugar in the tumbler. The customs duty on porter is heavy, I believe, as in Siberia a pint bottle costs a rouble and a half, or four shillings.

Another curious and unpleasant custom is, that when you are quietly taking your dinner, continual glasses of champagne may be brought you by the waiter, saying that Ivan Ivanovitch, or some other "vitch" wishes to drink your health, the sender being one of your acquaintances who is drinking at another table. Russian etiquette compels the acceptance of this attention.

The Siberians are extraordinary people to spend money in these restaurants when they are on a spree. While I was there, one gentleman commenced, and remained in the place for a whole week; at the end of that time his bill amounted to about two thousand roubles—three hundred pounds. On these occasions champagne corks are popping all day long, the contents of

ARRIVAL AT SIBERIAN POST-HOUSE.

To face p. 238.

the bottles being guzzled by any one who happens to come in.

The Siberian restaurants have one good custom, which our English keepers of similar houses would do well to follow. There is a garde-robe in the hall, where a man receives your overcoat, stick, and hat, giving you a cheque for them.

After dining with another Englishman in this restaurant, we came to the conclusion that there was not much difference, after all, between the Café Anglais at Paris and Plotnikoff's restaurant, at Ekaterienberg.

PEASANT WOMEN.

CHAPTER XXXV.

FAIRS.

THE annual fairs are a favourite source of amusement for the lower orders.

I must beg the reader to suppose he has accompanied me to the Easter fair in Moscow. This is held in a large open space called the "Podnavinskoi," we shall see there much to show us the sort of entertainment the mujik delights in.

The first thing that impresses a stranger, is the

ancient appearance of everything around him, he can scarcely believe he is moving in the present age, for the whole scene belongs rather to the seventeenth than the nineteenth century.

There are the usual "roundabouts," rings of flying horses, punch-and-judy shows, &c., as are common in all fairs.

The gentleman who is vaunting the praises and wonderful feats of his trained animals, will, you may be sure, make himself scarce before the performance commences; as in place of the lions, tigers, and black men that should be on view according to the flaming placards outside, a few cats, or at most a performing dog, will be all the patient and enduring mujik will see for his copeck.

Then again, there is a pretentious-looking wooden building, with its painted sign of "Pantomim from Lonon,"—a great attraction. On entering the building, the visitor will find it pretty comfortably arranged, and will be entertained with a sort of dumb burlesque, very broad and very stupid; but being from "Lonon," of course, the correct thing: the hero of the piece will be dressed as a mujik, whilst the heroine has donned the dress of Ophelia.

The next character we meet with is worthy of notice. A cunning-looking old mujik, with that peculiar grin on his face, which he assumes when he knows he is cheating you without the chance of detection, has a little tray suspended from his neck, on which is displayed a pack of the smallest of cards, which he continually manipulates: he does a large business, and is taking quantities of copecks from the boys. The children are his only customers, and they cannot resist the temptation of the chance of winning the exhibited rouble for their one-copeck stake. This, however, must take a considerable outlay, and a long time to accomplish; as, for curiosity, in the morning I noted the number of his bank-note, and here in the evening I find it is the same, so all this day the innings have been all in the old man's favour.

The next exhibition is also a novelty to an Englishman. On a platform, having a cover to protect the performer from the weather, stands a man, *got up* with plenty of white hair, to give his otherwise leery appearance a sage and old expression : his occupation is making impromptu jokes, generally of the broadest description, on the gaping crowd at his feet; reciting tales of at least questionable morality, accompanied always with lavish praise of the powers that be. His remuneration is entirely of the voluntary description, and generally drawn from the pockets of those whom he has obliged with his notice.

Many stalls, particularly for the sale of nuts, are to be seen, the traditional gingerbread not appearing to be known. Russians like to have their hands employed, and when not engaged at what the Americans call " whittling " wood with their axe, their next best employment is in diving into their pockets for nuts and sunflower seeds.

Toys, as usual in all fairs, take up a good deal of attention, and consume much time in the buying. A rouble will be asked for an article which you will ultimately get for a ten-copeck piece, but the process of bargaining is slow, though it appears to be entered into with much zest by both sides.

There are also exhibitions of wax-work so called, which on examination turn out to be made of wood.

The conjuror is not bad. He deals more in what he terms the " black art " than magic, and is much given to the snake and fire-swallowing business. This always takes greatly with the Russians.

In the booth yonder, where singing is going on, the performers are the choir from some church, who have come to earn an honest penny apart from their regular duties.

The building that we now enter is always crammed, for the entrance is free, the profit being derived from the sale of vodka and comestibles, in the shape of dainty pieces of bullock's liver, salt fish, &c., delicacies much prized by the lower orders. The amusement and *draw* here provided, are bands of dancers, performing national dances, in which the spectators, largely composed of servants, will join.

One or two of the large shows will be devoted to illustrating the glories of the Russian arms, particularly referring to Turkey and Circassia.

On the immense illustrated advertisement outside one of these shows is seen, one Russian soldier rescuing a princess from the citadel of a Turkish town. He is fighting his way out triumphantly over the bodies of some ten or a dozen Turks, whom he has killed. How, is not very apparent, as his sword is in its scabbard; for the best of all reasons, that, while one arm clasps the princess, the other holds a bag with SR. 50,000 written on it. Considering the weight of such an amount of specie, I imagine the artist means the contents of the bag to be paper, although the few hundreds of roubles the soldier has dropped in his flight are seen to be gold. Out come the actors for a parade before the next performance; a miserable lot they are; half-dressed, or rather undressed, they huddle themselves into line, men and women including the princess, whilst the clown tries to be funny: it is hard work even for him to make himself laugh, much more the outsiders, as the sleet has just begun to fall. Observe the warlike hero, poor wretch! half a Turk could swallow him whole. The crowd are not in an appreciating mood, so in the company tramps, to perform once more the " storming of Kars."

The sun shines again, and now it is the turn of the " conquerors of the Caucasus " to appeal to a confiding public, by showing them outside, gratis, a great proportion of the performance, which many have paid their copecks to see inside. Struck with their costume, we pay our fifty copecks, and enter the stalls to see the great military display.

Curtain rises to the music of a military band, and reveals the King of the Caucasus (who he was I am not quite clear) lamenting to his queen his old age, and expressing his desire to give his kingdom to the great benefactor of the universe — *the* Emperor; his wife rather coincides in the idea, but doubts whether *the* Emperor will be bothered by having it.   Enter a servant who announces the arrival of an envoy from Nicholas I., Emperor of the World.   The herald follows, escorted by troops (observe the dresses). The king is clothed like a Circassian, the herald as a mujik, and the guard of honour of the King

of the Caucasus are Russian firemen. The queen
is in an ordinary Russian dress.

As it appears to be contrary to etiquette in
these parts for the envoy to speak first, the king
asks him if he thinks his master the emperor
will consent to be troubled with his country and
people. The herald replies he will proceed to
St. Petersburg and inquire.

The royal pair then sit down to tea. In five
minutes the envoy returns — not having taken
too much time for his journey from the shores
of the Caspian Sea, where the scene is laid, to
St. Petersburg and back,—and announces to the
king that his master has acceded to his request,
and at the same time has been graciously pleased
to appoint the now ex-king a general in the
army, with the title of prince, at which intelligence the royal pair weep with delight, give a
great spread to the population, who appear to
be all Russians, and the curtain falls to the
sound of martial music and red fire.

All the principal booths have a military band,
or a portion of one, and as the signal for " going
to begin " is a loud bell, and as the various per-

formances are "going to begin" all day; what
with the incessant ringing and the discord of the
different bands playing at the same time, the
noise is overpowering.

The fair itself is exclusively for the lower
orders, but a peculiar feature is that the better
class of inhabitants drive round and round it
in carriages crammed with children for hours
together, for what reason it is impossible to
imagine.

The crowd in the fair was dense, but I saw
no row or disturbance, nor have I on any such
occasion. One cannot but be struck by observing what an order-loving people the Russians
are; and there were certainly not half as many
drunken specimens as would be seen at an
English fair.

There were plenty of police about, but they
were more busily engaged in looking at the
amusements than in interfering with the people.

In this scene, also, the natural politeness of the
lower orders can be studied. Watch that mujik
take off his hat, with the air and grace of a born
gentleman, and hear him say to his friend, who

is returning his salutation, " Ah ! Ivan Ivanovitch (meaning Mr. John), how is the health of
Maria Nicolaievna (Mrs. John) ?"   Amongst the
same class in England the salutation would be,
" Well, Jack, how's the missus ?"

Finally, one can walk about such a fair with
pockets safe from intrusive fingers the whole
time.

At a fair in a town in the Government of Vladimir, I saw a good specimen of the caricature
prints that were sold in the interior during the
Crimean war.

The walls of the traktirs were covered with
these ludicrous pictures. A peculiarity in them
was, that although Napoleon was always represented as the head of the French, Lord John
Russell did duty as his companion representing
the English interests.

In one picture these two are depicted crawling
up to the Emperor Nicholas, who is seated on his
throne in all the majesty of his glory. Allego-
rical tableau, I imagine, of the two nations suing
for pardon.

Another represents our Guards being inspected

before leaving for the seat of war.   All have pocket-handkerchiefs to their eyes.

A third shows the Imperial eagle soaring to the clouds, with Lord John in his clutches; the Emperor Napoleon, looking up in an attitude of dismay, curling his moustaches, as though he did not like the idea of Lord John going to glory at all.

At its side is a representation of a London street, crowded with John Bulls, who all have bulldog's heads on their shoulders, reading with looks of dismay the notice posted up announcing the "defeat of the allies on the banks of the Alma."

Several more caricatures were about, all of the same description.

It is only right to remark, however, that whatever opinions may have been entertained of us during the war, the feeling now is undoubtedly one of respect and regard for our nation.

CHAPTER XXXVI.

ПOTELS.

IN the capital towns of Russia there are some
good hotels, and no one can wish to be more
comfortably housed than in the Hotel de Russie,
kept by Herr Klee, in St. Petersburg, or in the
Hotel de Hambourg, kept by M. Billet, in Moscow; but when the traveller once gets away from
the large towns the accommodation becomes very
bad.

A comparatively short time ago there was not
a provincial hotel worthy of the name, and the
best thing a traveller could do was to content
himself with the accommodation which the post-
house placed at his disposal, namely, a warm

room, a table, a couple of chairs, and wooden
sofa; this latter, anyhow, had one advantage in
being made solid, and entirely of wood, the weary
traveller could sleep on it undisturbed by the
continual necessity of "going a hunting."

The means of locomotion being now greater,
a little improvement is to be observed, and in
such towns as Nijni Novgorod, Kief, Kazan,
&c., decent accommodation can be found, but
foreigners must not expect anything like comfort.

The conveniences are of the barest possible
description, and minus linen, unless particularly
ordered, and charged for extra. A Russian
generally travels with the sheets, towels, &c.,
he may require, and those who do not go
without.

When a Russian stays at one of these hotels,
he and his whole family take one room amongst
them, eating and drinking entirely from their
own stock of provisions; their tea and sugar
they always carry about with them, and the
more solid portions they purchase in the towns;
the only order they ever give to the hotel-
keeper is for the "samovar," or tea-urn, for

which a regular charge of ten copecks, or three pence, is made everywhere.

Such Russian families always have their servant with them, and he sleeps lying about somewhere in the passage outside his master's room; a bed is a luxury a Russian man-servant is seldom indulged with.

The aspect of a room-full, as I have described, is not desirable or pleasant, stuffed as it will be with adults and children, together with dirty clothes, furs, and sundry dishes of unused viands. I am bound to say, that in some of their habits, in travelling particularly, the Russians are pigs.

The use of water is only understood by them when they indulge in their weekly boil in the bath, so that in the hotels the accommodation for ablutionary purposes is of the most primitive description, and you may vainly search your room for a washing-stand.

For those luxurious people who require a wash in the morning, the waiter brings a small basin and jug of water, which, in order to economize, he will not pour out into the basin, but dribbles it over the hands drop by drop, whilst the person using it endeavours to refresh himself with this (as the waiter thinks) most extravagant consumption of water.

In case any of my readers should intend making a journey into the interior of Russia, I will relate for their edification a conversation I had with a waiter in the best hotel in a town in the central provinces.

I was shown to my room, which was of the usual uncomfortable description, the only thing in the shape of sleeping accommodation being an old sofa. I had no pillows, no linen with me; but, imagining that, as I was in a county town, I could get what I wanted for the asking, rang the bell for the waiter.

This functionary arrived, when I said, "Ivan, give me a pillow." "Seychass,"* replied the willing domestic, and presently returned with a most suspicious-looking bundle to act as my pillow. This turned out, upon examination, to be a quantity of dirty table-napkins, done up in a still dirtier table-cloth, and I felt constrained to decline it. I

---

* The waiter's "Yessir," literally, "This hour."

thought that I might perhaps get a sheet, and again asked the obliging Ivan to accommodate me. "Seychass," as usual, and he hurried away, only to return with a dirty table-cloth, and an apology that as the linen had gone to the wash, perhaps I could make that do instead of a regular sheet.

I made the best I could of it, and slept as I was. In the morning I undressed, intending to have a good wash, but for that I must have towels. "Now, Ivan, I suppose you can give me some towels?" "Of course, Excellency, sey-chass!" and this self-complacent waiter actually returned to me with the very same dirty table-cloth which he had already tried to palm off upon me as a pillow, as a sheet, and lastly as a towel.

CHAPTER XXXVII.

THE PROVINCIAL CLUB.

EVERY town of any importance has its club, which is generally styled the "nobility" club, as in the old time none but noblemen were eligible for admittance. Now the rule has been relaxed, and merchants are allowed to mix with aristocrats.

With the exception of the larger towns, the clubs are not generally open more than three days in the week, and it is only in the evening that anybody will be found in their saloons.

The first thing that strikes a stranger as being curious is the black board which he sees fixed on the wall at the top of the staircase. It is covered

with names, which have placed opposite to them
a sum of roubles, as, for instance,—

"Michael Michaelovitch Liboff, 2,345 S.R."
which means that Gospodin Liboff has lost in
the club 2,345 roubles, which he has not found it
convenient to pay to the friend who won it.

Any man playing at cards in a club is bound to
pay over his losings to the winner within a fixed
time, and if he does not do this, the winner has
the right to apply to the committee of the club to
have the defaulter's name posted on the black
board.

I believe that this right is very rarely exer-
cised, except in the case of a man who can pay
but won't pay.

Upon entering the club saloons, we observed
that every room was full of card-tables, not excepting the buffet-room where the eating goes
on, supper being generally taken at the club.

At present no games of chance are allowed to
be played. Preference and whist entirely engaged
the attention of the players, the marking being
all done on the table itself with white chalk.

Loto used to be the favourite occupation of all

visitors to clubs, but this led to such high gambling, joined in even by the women, that the Government stopped it.

In provincial clubs ladies are now generally admitted one day·in each week, when music is provided; and in the winter a regular feature is a fortnightly ball.

Ladies can and do play at cards at these clubs, mixing freely with the gentlemen.

Russians are very shy with whom they play at cards, and I fancy a good deal of "pigeoning" goes on.

Necessarily, from their numbers, a great majority of the visitors to the clubs are Tchinovniks and military men. The clubs are supposed to close at a certain hour, generally eleven or twelve, but the visitors can stay as long as they please by paying a fine for every quarter of an hour, which fine augments as each quarter passes. This forms a great source of revenue to these places.

The profit arising from the sale of cards is something immense, and is all received by the establishment for foundlings in Moscow, which has the sole right of selling cards all over the empire.

A curious feature in social life referring to cards is, that every one present at a party where they are played, on rising from the table pays twenty-five kopecks for the use of the cards, it being a perquisite of the servants to supply the packs and charge for those used at their master's table. A similar usage once held good in this country of England, I believe, as, if I recollect aright, one of the incidents in an old novel is the detection of a scoundrel stealing the coins placed under the foot of the candlesticks for the butler's fee.

But to return to the club.

Smoking is, of course, allowed in every room; and as the Russians always talk a great deal when they play, grumbling at and blowing up their partners for doing this and not doing that, the noise is sometimes frightful.

Tea is generally drank the whole time that play goes on. There is hardly any limit as to stakes, as people can be found to oblige you up to any point.

Large numbers of Russians are professed cardplayers, living upon the operation and doing nothing else. Many ladies gain a living in the same way.

The clubs are always crammed on the night of the day on which the local treasurer has paid the salaries of the Tchinovniks, who cannot omit a chance of increasing their " little all."

There is nothing particularly novel to be observed in the balls, as even there the men slink off to the card-tables. On these occasions the company is not particularly select, and ladies of all sorts mix pretty freely together.

Finally, provincial clubs are usually without reading-rooms, or newspapers—nothing but cards and smoke.

CHAPTER XXXVIII.

THE POLICE.

THE organization of the police in the towns differs materially from that in the villages.

The chief in the towns is called first police-master, and he has for assistants the second and third masters, these being the three persons who are responsible to the Governor for the proper behaviour of the place.

It is a curious fact that the police-masters of the larger towns, still adhere to the old-fashioned aristocratic style of equipage — a droschky with two horses, one in the shafts, and the other *dressé à volée* running loose at the side, whilst for other people this style has quite gone out of fashion.

These police-masters still have a good deal of power, and plenty of work to do. They hold a daily court, at which the chief presides, and at which they receive reports, complaints, &c. Before a foreigner can obtain a passport to go abroad, he must produce a certificate signed by one of the members of this court, that there is nothing " written-up against him ; " this is, however, only a necessary check in a country like Russia, for preventing people from running away in debt.

The common policemen are generally chosen from old soldiers, and dressed in a semi-military uniform with swords. They have small huts in the streets in which they live, and from which they do not often wander. The general amusement of a Russian policeman appears to be standing at his hut door, and occasionally taking a walk down the street for the purpose of seeing that the pavements and roads are kept clean. Breaches of the peace or street robberies are so rare that the police would find no employment did they only act as " guardians of the peace."

An important duty of the force is to see that the dvornik, or house-porter, is at his post, and properly attending to his charge, as it is this servant who is responsible to the police for the safety of the house, and in fact must receive a licence from them for the purpose, and so really acts as a sort of policeman.

The police are also used to serve notices, &c., and altogether their duties are multifarious.

They are a much better body of men than the old force were; are now generally well-behaved, and there are no private thrashings given by them, as used to be the case. Formerly, if a nobleman wished to pay out an Isvostchik, he would simply call up the first policeman he saw, give him three roubles, and tell him to give the unfortunate offender three roubles' worth of " stick."

It was customary for every householder to send a small present to the chiefs at Easter and Christmas, and this was a custom if not openly permitted, most certainly winked at by the ·

Government. The pay of these people has now been materially augmented, and if the custom still continues in some places, it is not tolerated by the Government but strictly prohibited.

The organization of the country police is a much more curious study.

The Governments or counties are divided into districts perhaps some sixty or eighty miles long, over each of which the governor of the province appoints an " Ispravnik " or chief of police, under him are two " Stanavoys," and these three between them have to look after the whole district. The work which these officials have to do is enormous; they are not only the guardians of the general peace, but they are the executors of the decisions of all the courts, as well as of the orders of the Governor, and the ukases of the Emperor. In point of fact they carry out all the Government business in their district, not forgetting the important duty of seeing to the collection of the Government taxes.

The " Ispravniks " are generally retired officers of about colonel's rank; their pay is now respectable, and they can live upon ·it. These men formerly amassed comfortable fortunes, but now, from my own observations, I am inclined to believe they are fairly honest.

The " Stanavoys " are a different class of men, and are generally chosen from among the Tchinovniks in the local towns. They are not much to be commended for the way they carry out their orders, and very often do not temper justice with mercy.

In the villages these officials have the " Starshina " to carry out the commands of the Governor or courts which are sent to them.

I have now to explain the most curious part of this organization. I have hitherto only described the heads of the country police, whose numbers naturally are not large.

It is the common policemen to whom the inhabitants of the villages look for protection, and these men are simply the village mujiks chosen by the Commune itself, and such a one is only to be distinguished from his brother by his brass badge and walking-stick.

As, therefore, only ten per cent. of the population of European Russia dwell in towns, ninety per cent. of the people rely for protection on "guardians of the peace" chosen by themselves.

I have already remarked that crime is not very frequent in Russia, and these village policemen are more often engaged carrying messages and papers to and from the towns than in attending to their other police duties.

. There is a force of gendarmes in the Empire, mounted, and almost exclusively engaged in keeping watch at the various railway-stations in the country, where two are always on duty.

I believe these men can be sent on police business about the country, but I have never seen them so employed.

In addition to the police forces I have described there is another organization, commonly called the " Secret Police." . It is the third division of the Imperial chancellerie, and has the most despotic powers in the cases of persons charged with political offences, but does not now meddle in ordinary criminal affairs.

IN A RUSSIAN VILLAGE.

To face p. 280.

The management of this third division has undergone great improvement during the last few years, but that such an establishment should exist in Russia is an event greatly to be deplored.

CHAPTER XXXIX.

COUNTRY PRISONS.

THE prisons of the Russian towns are all pretty much alike; they are usually situated in the immediate neighbourhood of one of the chief gates, or at some short distance in the outskirts. A gaunt, ugly-looking, stuccoed brick pile, surrounded with a palisade, having a couple of sentry-boxes standing perhaps fifteen or twenty yards in advance of the door in the centre of this wooden wall, shows the traveller he is before the county gaol.

Upon entering this building it will be found that the Russians divide their prisoners into two classes, "Ordinary" and "Secret." The former are confined in numbers together; the latter are kept on something resembling our solitary system : hence the name " secret," which has nothing whatever to do, as has been continually written, with political prisoners.

There is of course the women's " side," and the men's " side " in the prison.

Taking first the " Ordinary " class for my remarks, it does not seem to me that they suffer much hardship by their punishment. They are herded together in a large room, and have no compulsory employment or task-work of any kind. At night they sleep in the same place, not in beds, but on wooden reclining boards which run round the room.

They are well fed, have exactly the same food that they would have at home, namely stchee or cabbage-soup, cucumbers, dried fish, black bread, &c., and those that I saw seemed very comfortable. This class is confined to prisoners under remand for trifling offences, as well as those sentenced to short terms of imprisonment.

The discipline amongst this class appeared to me to be very lax; they seemed to be too well treated and to take it too easily, although on the whole the prison was well managed.

Those of the " secret " class who are very bad, are kept in solitary cells, though sometimes two or three are placed together. These separate cells, in the prison I am describing, were roomy, well ventilated and clean.

With the exception of soldiers as guards, and a few gaolers, the whole of the staff were prisoners. I should mention here, that these prisons are under the management of the provincial assembly.

As far as I could make out, the so-called " nobleman," when in prison, has the right of wearing his own clothes, instead of the ordinary prison dress; and this presumption is founded on the fact that I saw a man of this class confined on the solitary system. He had been convicted of a bad crime, but had appealed against the sentence passed on him, and was then awaiting the judgment of the superior court; meanwhile he was in his ordinary clothes, with many comforts, such as a good bed, and articles of furniture around him.

The superintendent of the prison informed

me that he had much more trouble to keep the women than the men in order.

Upon comparing the size of a prison with that of the town where it is situated, one would be led to suppose that crime must be very frequent in the Empire. This is not, however, the fact. Towns which are of sufficient importance to have prisons are few and far between, and must accommodate the prisoners from large districts.

The published statistics show that crime is not as frequent in Russia as in our western countries.

A very curious custom still exists and is practised upon those unfortunate wretches sentenced to penal servitude; the hair is shaved from one side the head. This is done, I believe, as a means of identification.

A BOKHARIAN AMBASSADOR.

CHAPTER XL.

A BOKHARIAN AMBASSADOR.

I MENTIONED in a previous sketch having met an individual on a steamboat at Kazan, who had attracted my attention by the curious manner in which he was hugging what I thought to be a brass water-jug, but which turned out to be a present intended for the Emperor.

I suppose Oriental grandees take a great deal of time for their journeys, for it was several months after I had first seen this gentleman, when I again encountered him on the road.

On returning from Siberia the winter was just commencing, and the roads were as hard as adamant, but as no snow had fallen, we were obliged to journey in our tarantass. This was not pleasant, and to complete our discomfort, somewhere on the road between Kazan and Nijny Novgorod, the axletree of the carriage broke, and we were thus obliged to stay all night on the spot; rather a disagreeable finish to a journey of several thousand miles.

In the morning, after having repaired the damage and when about to start again, a cavalcade of vehicles dashed past us, in one of which sat our old friend still hugging this precious jug. It was very ludicrous to watch this old man, as, with every jolt of the machine he was riding in, he was forced to make a corresponding effort to preserve his charge from being damaged.

We kept company on the road and arrived at Nijny Novgorod, where I thought they would surely stay and rest. However, upon arriving at the station, there the party were, staring with astonishment at the railway engines and carriages.

I watched them admiringly, with their sharp black eyes staring out from their copper-coloured skins, their fine countenances well brought out by the background of glossy jet-black hair, and turban of handsome shawl-patterned stuff; but I thought they all looked as though they would be much happier when they get back to their own infidel stronghold.

As the second bell rang, I entered a carriage, and the station being dark, I did not readily observe who my fellow-travellers were.

On leaving the dusk of the station for the somewhat better light of the open country, I perceived that my only companions were the Bokharians.

Their party of seven was composed of the old image of an ambassador, two assistants, a mollah, a reader, and two servants.

The mollah knew a little Russian, so that we managed to understand one another. But the old man could not make out meeting an English-man in that part of the world, and remarked, through his mollah, that he thought it was only to India that Englishmen ever wended their steps.

The time came for them to perform their devotions. They commenced by taking off their outer silk gowns, which they placed on the floor of the carriage as carpets, and knelt on them, without, as far as I could hear, saying much. They then stood up with their heads bowed, and appeared to be lost in thought. All kneeling down again, the mollah seemed to me to repeat a prayer, which being concluded, they rose with a shake, and this part of their devotions was finished. Getting into their gowns, they listened while the mollah read a portion of the Koran.

A short time then elapsed, when the reader again read to them, but this was some story or fairy tale, to which I observed the whole party paid more attention than to the Koran. After this the company generally prepared for a snooze.

The mollah did not turn out to be very communicative; and, like all Orientals, was chary of giving information.

The old man had a considerable difficulty with

his jug. He could not get it into a position which would let him sleep in comfort. Trying the floor, after his native custom, he found it very cold; but at last, having carefully wrapped up himself and his inseparable companion, he somehow managed to drop off soundly, as I was given to understand by his loud snoring.

The scene was so novel to me that I remained wide awake. The ambassador did not enjoy his repose undisturbed very long. The engine gave one of those long, loud whistles, to which every railway traveller is accustomed. Not so, however, was the old man; in his sleep he forgot he was in the land of the Christians, and up he jumped with any amount of cries to Allah to protect him.

At the next station he wanted to get out and go back; but he was persuaded to remain, and in the morning, upon learning we were nearing Moscow, where he had been informed some Imperial aide-de-camp would be waiting for him, he proceeded to dress fittingly for the occasion. His servants produced, from a very seedy-looking bundle, the old man's state-clothes, which he very coolly exchanged for those he had on, entirely ignoring the Christian's presence. His costume was completed by placing a splendid belt of gold, profusely studded with precious stones, round his waist; but this, like the jug, the old man had himself guarded carefully, by keeping it in his own pocket.

At Moscow station I bid him good-bye, and do not suppose I shall ever again see this Bokharian ambassador.

CHAPTER XLI.

DOMESTIC SERVANTS.

I MUST admit that servants are a great trouble in Russia, although they have redeeming features which make up for some of their short-comings.

Servants are rarely engaged from verbal characters, but have always what are called their " attestats " with them. These being written, really go for nothing, as in the old time if a master wrote a bad character on them, the servant would have him up before the police, notwithstanding that the law was compulsory regarding an attestat, if the servant required it. I got over the difficulty by simply writing, " Ivan or Mascha came into my service on the 1st of January, 1870, and left it on the 12th of April, 1870."

The servants hate doing housework, such as scrubbing or washing, and a contract has to be made with people outside the house, to come once or twice a week to scrub and clean the rooms.

Men-servants are almost invariably used for waiting, and if a good cook is required, a man must be engaged. All the cooks get drunk, and almost all are thieves in their department. On great occasions or high holidays it is a rare thing for them to be sober. In the country we usually took the precaution to lock the cook up at those times, to prevent the chance of our going dinner-less.

We had a very curious man once; he was our cook in the country, and I took him up to town. He was a capital cook, but an awful fellow to drink. In the country, when he got too bad, he was sent to the mayor to get mildly thrashed, and so we managed to keep him in a passable state; but when he got to town,

where thrashing is not the custom, he got out-
rageous.

One day he came home very drunk, and began
smashing the windows. I sent for a policeman,
and on his way to the lock-up, thinking he was
in the village in the hands of the "Sotsky," he
called out, "Never mind, the director is only
sending me to the mayor to be thrashed! I
don't care for a *thrashing*, it's the *fines* I don't
like." However, this gentleman altered his tone
and demeanour before the judge, and was very
delighted at being allowed to escape to his village
again.

The women make wonderful nurses, and I
don't suppose any child gets more undivided
attention than the little charge of a Russian
nurse.

I know of no servants who fall into the ways
of their masters so quickly as the Russians,
and they are not much trouble in the way of
living, though requiring a table of their own;
this, however, is supplied very cheaply and
moderately. Their wages are comparatively
small, so that the many domestics necessary in

Russia are not nearly so expensive as the few with us.

Servants are invariably hired by the month, but their services can be dispensed with, and they can also leave their employer, at three days notice.

The sleeping accommodation, which might be supposed a serious consideration in a large household, gives little concern to the master. The cook as often sleeps atop of a cupboard in his kitchen, as he does anywhere else, whilst the rest of the domestics stretch themselves at length in the long passages or the warmest corners they can find.

In towns, every house has to employ a servant called a " Dvornik " or door-keeper. The duties of this man are peculiar, for besides doing some little house-work, such as carrying wood and water, he is the medium of communication with the police in giving notice of the arrival of strangers at the house, and having all the passports registered with the commissary of the district. This functionary also acts as watchman, and has a little room or shed to live in, in the yard of the house.

Coachmen are always chosen for the length of their beards and stoutness of their bodies.

The master of the house always holds the passports of all his servants as a check against their running away whilst in his employ.

CHAPTER XLII.

CONSTANTINOPLE AND SAINT SOPHIA.

I AM not going to horrify my readers with a disquisition upon politics, as they might fancy from the title of this sketch.

I have always believed that Russia must one day have Constantinople, as, leaving alone all questions such as — the gathering together of the Slave family with the Czar of Russia as their head — the rights of race — fighting for the independence of people, &c.—which eighty per cent of the population neither understand, nor care about, the universal feeling among all the Russian people who know that there is such a place as

Constantinople is that the place belongs to Russia, and that one day they must have it.

To illustrate this feeling, I cannot do better than relate the following anecdote told me by one of the parties mentioned in it.

One of the largest and richest merchants in the Empire, a man who counts his fortune by millions, had two sons to whom he wanted to give the advantage of travel : he secured the services of a distinguished Professor of the University of Kazan, and giving him an unlimited credit, sent his sons abroad under his care to visit the world.

Two years of travel over, they returned, and the Professor presented to the father two polished young gentlemen.

" Well," said the father, addressing the professor, " where have you been — to Constantinople ? " " No." " To America ? "   " Yes." " Have you seen the President ? "   " Yes." " Seen the Pyramids ? "   " No."

" Well, I am not astonished," replied the father, " that you have not seen the Pyramids, but I cannot understand why you have not shown my sons *our* Saint Sophia."

CHAPTER XLIII.

A BEAR HUNT.

RUSSIANS are not a sporting people, and it is only the bear that gives them anything like a desire for a hunt.

If a mujik can only find Bruin in his winter quarters, he is happy, as it gives him that which he loves so much—a " pot " shot.

There are always one or two peasants in every neighbourhood who spend the winter in searching for bear-holes, primarily with the idea of selling the " find " to some neighbouring gentleman or, if that fails, by making a few roubles out of the animal's skin and fat.

The operation of searching is difficult, and even dangerous: the snow is so extremely fine and soft that walking on it without snow-shoes is impossible, and these, long narrow slips of wood turned up at the ends, with a piece of leather nailed across the middle into which to place the feet, are difficult things to manage. Going on level ground is easy enough, but up or down hill the wearer of them is very apt to tumble; and then, with some three feet of shoe sticking into the snow, and head and arms deeply plunged by the force of the fall, extrication is a work of time, and partial suffocation a close probability.

When, therefore, we have discovered a bear to be "at home," we let him alone until the snow is on the eve of disappearing, and he can be comfortably approached. By that time, also, he will be waking up from his hibernation, and a little more lively than he would be if we roused him in the midst of his winter slumbers.

My greatest adventure in bear-hunting came about in the following manner. I was accustomed to pay a reward of five-and-twenty roubles to the man who found me a bear, and this reward kept my peasants on the look-out.   The first mujik who, towards the end of a long winter, came to claim it one fine morning, lived at a distance of some hours' drive from my house.   We drove over to his village to arrive towards evening, and sat down to supper in his house, where the head forester met me.   After supper we cleared out the mujik and his family, and settled down, my head forester and I, to go to sleep.   Oh ! what a night that was !   I was tired from my long drive, and really wanted sleep; but had no sooner closed my eyes than down *They* began to troop on me from the ceiling, and from the walls, from the joints of the rude bench which I laid upon; from the planks of the floor they began to swarm, and every sensitive part of my limbs and body to "prate of their whereabouts."   The Russian species has a peculiarly tingling and poisonous bite, and before ten minutes of their attack had been sustained, the forester and I gave up sleep as a hopeless thing.   Now the forester being great in this branch of entomology, set to improving the occasion with a lecture on the *cimex*

lectularius, pointing out to me how we had to do
with a black sort, of peculiar voracity, and not
with either of the two large brown varieties,
which, however nasty, don't bite.

Hours before daylight we were on our way
to the forest, the snow had begun to melt, and
the road was rough for sledging, especially here
and there where we come to bare places where
the snow was destroyed by tepid springs.   I
have forgotten to mention these hot springs
before, but they are very common in some parts
of Russia.

The jolting of the sledge was unpleasant, and
so far the journey was a disagreeable one. But
the coral magnificence of the ancient forest com-
pensated for bodily discomfort.   No man of observation can pass these primæval forests without
discovering wonders at every turn.   The monster
trees—whose thick trunks and arms are twisted
into fantastic distortions, darken the road with
the thick caverns they form where the wind
has uprooted them by dozens, and they lean
supported by their branches across the way—
seen in the grey morning as we glide along our

silent path of snow, have a solemn and imposing influence on the mind, like that produced by the ruins of some grand old temple, whose foundation, like that of our Russian forest, is hidden in remote antiquity.

When we left our sledge and took to struggling through the wood, we sank deep in the snow at every step, and were thoroughly glad to arrive at last before the winter residence of our bear. The air-holes left for breathing purposes in the snow were freshly discoloured, and showed that Bruin was at home: so we got to business without delay.

Shooting a bear as he emerges from his winter quarters is not unattended with danger, because, if the shots do not happen to be mortal, the animal charges, and the men near the hole are sometimes knocked over and mauled.

It is very necessary, therefore, that the shooter should be supported by a man with a spear, who stands close behind him and receives the bear, in case of need on the point of his weapon. This duty can only be entrusted to an old hand, and one who never flinches.

Besides the gun which the shooter carries in his hand, he must have a second in reserve behind him, as bears sometimes take a great deal of killing.

The battery being supposed to be arranged, the mujiks begin to call and talk to the bear. If this does not move him they insert a small tree, and literally "stir him up with the long pole." The animal then (generally in a drowsy state) puts his head through the opening, and upon presenting a fair mark is killed. But if he is already awake in his hole before the stirring up process commences, he will bolt out with a rush which is far from agreeable.

On the occasion I am referring to we had made a mistake in our calculations, for after all the bear had given us the slip; but we knew that he could not be far off, as he had only left his hole a few minutes before. We accordingly separated to hunt him up. I was walking amongst the brushwood with a man behind me carrying a spare double-barrelled rifle, when I heard the bear growl, but could not see him; presently I made him out about thirty or forty

BRUIN AROUSED.

To face p. 290.

paces off, and looking round to see that my other gun was near, beheld the fellow carrying it, in the act of making off as fast as he could. I caught him up and made him stand, and in the mean time the bear was slowly advancing towards us. There was so much underwood that I could not see to make a sure shot, but at last was obliged to fire. The rifle I had in my hand was an English Enfield. I missed the shoulder and struck the brute in the side. I found afterwards that the ball had gone through him, literally riddling him. He took no notice of this beyond giving a growl. He then came towards me, when I took my second gun, and fired point-blank at his forehead; the gun was a smooth-bore and the bullet round; this also had no effect on him beyond causing just a shake of his head and another growl. I had only one barrel left, and did not like the situation, as my spearman was hunting on his own account and had not yet come up; but I for the first time in my life learned by experience the full value of a breech-loader, for I had just time to put a cartridge in the empty barrel, giving me two more chances, when the animal was almost close to me. Stepping aside, I fired into his heart, and he fell dead at my feet. This was a lesson to me in the future not to depend upon myself alone in attempting to kill a bear.

CHAPTER XLIV.

MEAT AND DRINK.

THE fashionable people in the large towns of Russia eat and drink the same food, in the same manner, as is usual in all large capitals: it is only therefore with the other classes that we have to do in this chapter.

To commence with the mujik, whose fare is very simple. Cabbage-soup to-day with a change to mushroom ditto to-morrow, a heavy allowance of black rye-bread, and as a dainty some buck-wheat dished up in oil, make up his ordinary *cuisine*. The little etceteras are a very small sort of cucumber, something like our gherkins, eaten fresh in summer, and pickled in salt and water in winter; and in fast times, all sorts of fishes are eaten—it is quite immaterial to the people what they are. Many are caught in the neighbouring ponds, and are just common white fish, whilst the larger quantity come from the rivers Volga and Don, as well as from some of those in Siberia.

During the winter time as well as in the fasts a great deal of oil is consumed; the peasants are not very particular as to quality, and whether made from hemp, rape, or sunflower seed, it is all one to them. Potatoes are not generally eaten by the mujiks, and are called by them "Devil's apples."

The poor abused mujik has been constantly described as an individual who drinks nothing but vodka, whilst the truth is, that his general drink is water, and as a treat on great days qvass, a liquor made of fermented rye, the vodka-drinking only coming in on the holidays.

Meat is a thing the mujik rarely sees, and when he does indulge in such a delicacy, it is generally in the shape of a piece of liver, or a cow's heel, or some other extraordinary part that nobody else cares about: the little bit of solid stuff bought invariably going into the soup-pot.

All Russians are inordinate consumers of salt, —a good thing for the Government, there being a heavy tax upon that article.

It can easily be understood from the foregoing description of his fare that the mujik cannot be a strong man. Whether his abstinence has arisen from his poverty or his church discipline, I know not; but I am inclined to think from the latter, as there are more than 200 days in the year on which he must not eat meat.

Rising up a step in the social scale, we find much the same sort of diet as a foundation, with several auxiliaries.

The merchant or middle class keep to their black bread, their qvass, and the cabbage-soup, which on their tables, however, has plenty of meat in it. They eat the buckwheat and the cucumbers, but supplement all this with joints of meat and vegetables. Amongst the edibles consumed by this class are to be found dainties worthy of imitation. At the commencement of the winter for instance, nothing can be conceived more appetizing in conjunction with a joint of roast meat, than a pickled apple, that is to say an apple which has laid for some time in water fermented by rye-bread. Peaches are preserved by these people in a manner which in my opinion has no equal. Mushrooms, and a variety of other species of fungi, red, yellow, brown, and black, are cooked in a manner which now when I write this makes my mouth water.

Besides qvass; mead and a sort of beer called brüga are also in common use amongst this class.

The highest country class of noblemen have the same fare, with still more additions, such as the choicest kinds of smoked fish, good cheeses, quantities of game, and a variety of wines; but in spite of these delicacies at their command, they still adhere to the national tschee, buckwheat and qvass.

The Russian cooks of the better sort are usually men, and excel in making all sorts of pastry and confectionary. Nothing can be richer than the creams and ices made by these " artists."

Some most remarkably piquant and delicious

relishes must be noted. Caviare eaten fresh (it is so delicate that even in St. Petersburg itself it is impossible to obtain it quite fresh) on a piece of a Moscow kalash (a kind of hot white bread) with the sensation of a spring onion scraped upon it, is a treat for a gourmand which is not to be obtained in any other country; whilst preserved caviare, similar to that which is seen here, is about as disagreeable oily stuff as it is possible to imagine. The sterlet I have already described. Some of the pickled mushrooms are especially fine. A Russian double-snipe shot upon the corn-fields at the end of August, exceeds in flavour any game I have ever tasted, whilst a cold " Rabchick " or tree-partridge, eaten with a cucumber after being one day in brine, is a dish fit for a king.

Several sorts of native-grown wines are now used, much of which comes from the banks of the Don, but the major part from the Crimea. These wines are cheap and extremely palatable, a bottle of either red or white may be obtained retail for forty copecks or about a shilling.

Some foreign luxuries are to be obtained in

Russia of a very superior quality, noticeably champagne and cigars. After my taste the *carte blanche* of Roederer and the brand of Cliquot (both manufactured expressly for Russia) are not to be equalled, whilst the *ne plus ultra* cigars of Upman, are most certainly not to be matched elsewhere than in Cuba.

In fact, the general living in Russia, excluding that of the mujik, is not bad. It is perhaps a little too unsubstantial and farinaceous to quite suit our more Western ideas, but it is on the whole very supportable. There is a little too much grease in the cookery to be altogether pleasant, and in this the mujik revels.

I remember once calling the attention of one of the footmen to the candle which was not properly fixed into the candlestick. He very simply righted the matter by taking the candle out, putting it into his mouth, and biting half an inch off, which he swallowed and seemed to enjoy; whilst to show that the mujiks are not particular as to what they drink, I can narrate the fact of a man in a town being nearly ruined through the following.

He had made a contract to light a suburb with petroleum ; one morning, however, he came to the director of the department with a very long face, and announced the fact that he must give up his contract and forfeit the hand-money paid.

" Why, Ivan, do you want to give up your contract? I thought the price of petroleum was going down," said the director.

" Yes, so it is," responded Ivan ; " it is not the price that frightens me."

" Then what is the matter?" asked the impatient director.

" Why you see, excellency, as fast as I put the petroleum in the lamps, the pigs of mujiks come and drink it."

On another occasion in our house in the country, a bottle of Gregory powder got broken, and the contents were being swept up by an English servant to be thrown away, when up came one of the Russian men-servants, and remarked, that it was a pity to waste it: might he have it ?

" Certainly ; but what will you do with it ?— it is medicine."

"Never mind that," said the man, "I'll take it home."

The next morning Ivan was asked what he had done with the powder?

"Why, I made it into a pudding," was his reply.

Out of charity for the feelings of his family and himself, we did not ask him concerning the sequel.

CHAPTER XLV.

GERMANS IN RUSSIA.

I HAVE said that the Russian people do not love the Germans, and whilst I cannot help admitting that the peasant had in the olden time good reason for the sentiment, it must be owned that the Teutonic race has done a vast amount of good in the Russian empire. In the capital the majority of the large shopkeepers are German, whilst in the few other large towns in the Empire many Germans are engaged in trade.

At St. Petersburg, by far the wealthiest bankers, merchants, and brokers, are Germans, and many more are of German origin. Commencing from the time of Catherine, the English for many years kept the majority of the trade in their hands; they have been, however, quite distanced by the Germans, and the English are now comparatively nowhere.

But it is in the country that these industrious and frugal people have set an example to the Russian mujik, of which I am sorry to say he has not taken advantage.

Scattered here and there over the Empire are German colonies; some of them, established many years ago upon land given to them by the Crown, have gradually grown into great importance. In several of them manufactories have sprung up, and generally they are industrious and prosperous.

It is quite curious in passing through such a colony to notice the nice houses, clean streets, well-kept fields, everything after the German type, and quite different from the Russian-owned property which it may join. In fact, there is Germany in the middle of Russia.

I have often mentioned that the mujiks are very monkeys for imitation, but it is a great pity that they have not copied the Germans in their manner of cultivating the land.

CHAPTER XLVI.

THE OLDEN TIME.

THE story contained in this sketch brings so vividly to my mind the difference betwcen the Russia of to-day and that of the olden time, that I have been induced to insert it as the concluding anecdote of this book.

It has been circulated before, but this is the first time, I believe, that the whole truth is published. The facts were related to me by one of the parties concerned, and as all interested arc now dead I feel myself free to detail them.

In the olden time the Government paid its servitors so badly, that no man calculated the actual sum of his salary, but invariably looked at what his income might be made to amount to.

To such an extent was this system of robbery resorted to, that no secret whatever was made of the means by which the end was accomplished; as everybody received, so everybody expected, and I have myself caught the keeper at my park-gates taking copecks from the poor mujiks, before he would allow them to enter with their petitions, and this process would be repeated by every doorkeeper or servant the poor devil had to pass. It was no wonder that this system reigned rampantly throughout the Empire: that the man with the pocket prospered, while the man without, and the occasional honest fellow that was to be met with, went to the wall.

The roads and the bridges required repairing and renovating; the order would be given for the necessary materials, but if my reader had happened to be on that unfortunate road which was supposed to have consumed these materials, his eyes would have been sorely tried in looking for the improvements; rather let him have followed

the movements of the " Polkovnik" or Colonel
in command of the particular district, and he
would very probably have found out that the
same colonel was building a nice house for himself in the neighbouring town, to which the
materials had been consigned.

But all these swindles were bagatelles compared to the proceedings when the railroads first
began to be built. And it is referring to them
that I write this sketch.

The Emperor Nicholas was desirous of connecting the two capitals—viz., St. Petersburg and
Moscow—by a railway.

Many curious circumstances occurred during
the building of this road. On one occasion a
high official wished to go over a portion of it,
to see what a Russian railway was like. An
engine was ordered to be in attendance at a
certain hour to take the visitor: at the appointed
time, however, no engine was to be seen. Where
was it ? was asked by all, and telegram after
telegram was sent down the line already finished,
to demand this unfortunate engine. " If you
cannot send the one I ordered send another,"

telegraphed the infuriated and perplexed engineer. However, no engine came, and there was a pretty row.

Next day the superintendent went down the line to find the engine, he returned without any success.

A certain number of engines had been received, paid for, and delivered to the railway, and had subsequently been taken to pieces, bit by bit, stolen, and sold, no one knew by whom.

This was rather refined stealing. Another mode, not so neat, was the following:—The line as built was paid for at a calculation per verst; when it was finished, the verst-posts seemed placed very close together. Hints were freely thrown out that the road was only some six hundred and fourteen versts long, whereas considerably more than that number of distance-posts figured on the way. This led to a re-measuring, when the truth came out, that the Government had paid for many more versts than were actually made.

In short, the plunder on this job was immense,

and rumour connected with the scandal the names of men high in office and in the confidence of their sovereign.

If report speaks truly, the system of jobbery had by this time culminated to such a pitch, that few names were free from association with some piece of rascality or other; and the names of ministers even were freely bandied about from mouth to mouth as participators in the profit derived from some of the more noted of these cases.

No one knew better than the Emperor Nicholas himself the ways of his *employés*, but even he could not alter this state of things.

It has been hinted that he even encouraged his civil servants in exacting their incomes from his subjects; but surely Nicholas had far too educated and refined a mind to tolerate such a contemptible way of earning a livelihood.

In many ways I think the character of Nicholas was much misunderstood. Firm and exacting in his ideas of duty; impetuous and even rough in his temper; when thwarted, passionate to a degree for the moment; not brooking the assertion of any opinions against his own; with the most autocratic of autocratic ideas, he was of a most refined mind; had a charitable heart towards the distress of others; the most elegant tastes of a highly-educated man; and moreover he was one, who, Emperor as he was, was never ashamed to acknowledge that he had been wrong, when upon reflection he had felt himself to have been mistaken. He was a man who had in himself capital business ideas, and upon every account it would appear that Nicholas could not willingly have allowed such confusion to exist in his government.

There were two ministers, at the time I am speaking about, who were supposed to be more intimately acquainted with the system of peculation than anybody else, and who had suddenly become very rich. The Emperor had had many hints thrown out to him as to the manner in which these riches had been amassed. The enormous cost his railway had been to his exchequer, the great increase in the issue of bank-notes, were alike pointed out as being not improbably the means by which these great fortunes had been realized.

It was of no avail : the ministers retained their portfolios, and the scandal remained on everybody's tongue.

Another minister, who was as honest as he was clever, feeling very indignant at the rascality which he believed was practised, hit upon the following mode of conveying his ideas to his Majesty.

Nicholas had intimated to this minister that he intended paying him a visit on a certain day. The day arrived, and with it came the Emperor.

It was the custom then, as it is now, for every one holding a superior position under the Government, to have a portrait of the reigning monarch hanging in his saloon, or grand reception-room.

This portrait generally hangs on the wall at the end of the chamber facing the door, and enjoys the honour of being hung in solitary grandeur, as it is not etiquette to surround it with other pictures.

For this occasion, before the Emperor arrived,

the master of the house added two companion-
portraits, one hanging upon either side of the
Emperor's.

The portraits were those of the two ministers
who were not loved by the host.

Nicholas arrived, and on entering the saloon,
immediately noticed the change that had been
made. He chatted with the master of the house,
but was evidently ill at ease, though too polite
to make any allusions to the decided breach of
etiquette that his eagle eyes had so quickly
observed, and remained quiet on the subject.
In time other guests arrived, and remarking what
had been done, began to whisper among themselves. The Emperor could not understand the
meaning of all this, and at last, taking his host
aside, said,—

" I see you have been making some alteration
in your picture-gallery."

" Yes, Sire," responded the nobleman; "I
have been amusing myself to-day by arranging
my idea of *a tableau of the Crucifixion.*"

It is asserted that this little episode accomplished the desired end, and that one at least of

the ministers implicated immediately sent in his resignation ; but it is perfectly certain that the nobleman who arranged this novel mode of " putting the question," retained the intimate friendship of Nicholas until his death.

CHAPTER XLVII.

CONCLUSION.

IN the foregoing sketches of some of the phases of Russian life, manners, and customs, my object has been to endeavour to portray the character of the people from a point of view not attainable by the ordinary traveller, or, in fact, by the resident in the towns.

Town life and country life in Russia are very different. The inhabitants of the two capitals, St. Petersburg and Moscow, are to a great extent cosmopolitanised, and the former city can hardly to-day be called a Russian town. In it many of the Russian inhabitants have caught the foreign tone, and live a foreign life, and adopt foreign manners and customs, while in the country and the country towns, the inhabitants have not yet had the advantage of rubbing against foreigners, but remain with their manners and customs, not simply Eastern, as is very often attributed to them, but essentially, with ways and manners of their own—Russian.

The bygone life which I have depicted was not a cheerful picture to look upon; in fact, nothing could be more at variance with everything we have been taught to regard as right and proper, than the ancient *régime* of the Russian people.

The conservatism and obstinacy of the ancient nobility had, I believe, no equal in the world. The manner in which the people were treated by them has not been exaggerated by me in the least; and I have shown this phase of character the more willingly, in order that my readers may fully appreciate the great changes and improvements which have been given to the nation.

It is very difficult to comprehend how it came to pass that Russia remained so long behind the world in matters of reform and progress; but since the year 1861 her strides in the onward path have been immense. Necessarily much has still to be done, but at the same time, with a knowledge of the difficulty that must have been experienced in carrying the established reforms out, it is really wonderful that so much has been accomplished in the time.

The head of the State, by surrounding himselt with men not only honest, but capable, has been enabled to do more for his people than has perhaps ever been permitted to be done by any one sovereign.

The reforms already carried out would, if they were chronicled in all their fulness, fill volumes, and it is quite impossible to speak of them all; for really to appreciate them a person should have lived under the old *régime* and the new.

The emancipation of the serfs, by which many millions of human beings were freed from tyranny and oppression, and obtained the right of citizenship, naturally called for the other reforms which followed soon after in the steps of what was, after all, only a simple act of justice.

The new law, with its simple code, its oral instead of written practice, trial by jury, irremovable judges,—elected by the supreme power instead of by the local nobility, and withal well paid,—was a boon to a people who before this gift had no other law except that of money.

A class of gentlemen educated as advocates, and influenced by the same high tone of morality that distinguishes our bar, is an invaluable addition to the wants of the Russian litigants of the present day.

Formerly, the priestly office was hereditary. No one could be a Pope whose father had not been so before him; now, anybody willing and able to pass the necessary examination can become a member of the priestly circle. It can fairly be presumed, then, that the fathers-Peter are making way for a more intelligent and enlightened class.

Local self-government is introduced: thus all have a share in the distribution of taxes which they pay.

The position of the press has been ameliorated. The same system of *avertissement* exists as in

Austria and France, and although many notices are given, politics are pretty freely discussed, and the tone has, in consequence, increased in respectability and importance. With a dynasty as secure as the present one, and loved so much by the people at large, it is impossible to understand why there are any restrictions on the press whatever. A new law on the freedom of the press is promised, and its introduction is looked forward to with much interest.

The Russian tariff was the worst in Europe; the protective duties and the conservative ideas regarding home-manufactures were detestable. The latest alterations, however, ameliorated this state of things, and the present tariff, although not a Birmingham one, is much better than its predecessor.

The introduction of the railway system throughout the Empire is by no means one of the latest improvements that we have seen during the last double lustre; for surely railways mean an increase of intelligence and prosperity.

The reforms in the management of the departments of the different branches of the civil service, if not yet complete, show such an improvement upon the rottenness and dishonesty which used to be the distinguishing marks of these bureaux, that the time cannot be far distant when this reform will be complete.

The treatment of the soldier has been greatly ameliorated. The knout and " running the gauntlet " are traditions of the past.

The fact that the navy is under the administration of the Grand Duke Constantine, is sufficient to show that the condition and welfare of the common sailor are carefully and disinterestedly attended to.

That the absorbing question of education has not been neglected, is proved by perhaps the last of the reforms introduced; namely, — that one making the classics a part of the general educational scheme. A great opposition was made to this innovation, but the point was carried by the Minister of Public Instruction.

The mujik, who for years was purposely kept by his Barrin in a state of ignorance, has now the opportunity afforded him of giving an education to his children.

Travelling is now free and unimpeded throughout the Empire; the necessity for the production of a passport at every turn of the traveller's progress is abolished, and once *in* the Empire, for the purpose of travel, the passport never need be shown.

Gas and water works are to be seen in towns which a few years ago were in darkness, and without the means of a necessary supply of the cleansing element. Streets, which were a sea of mud, are paved; and stone bridges have been built across the rivers which formerly only boasted of a water-way from shore to shore.

The telegraph now flashes the news from one end of this large kingdom to the other, and to-day it is as easy to speak from Perm to New York, as a short time ago it was from St. Petersburg to its suburbs.

A middle class of people, large in number and powerful in means, is fast appearing, who will have much to say and do in the future development of their country; and yet only ten years have elapsed since the commencement of its formation. Until the year eighteen hundred and sixty-one, there were only two classes of people in the Czar's dominions—nobles and serfs. Now there are four—noblemen, merchants, shop-keepers, and peasants.

The viciousness of the aristocracy is passing away, and those of them who wish to hold their own see the necessity of conforming to the new state of affairs. The young men of this class now pay attention to their home matters and their own interests, and do thereby much good to themselves, their people, and their country.

Of the more ordinary advancements which are the result of the above reforms, that of the budget is the most important.

In a pamphlet, which I published in Moscow in 1869, I drew attention to the rapid manner in which the finances of the Empire were im-proving, and to the fact that the budget of receipts was gradually yet surely approaching to the expenditure. It is very satisfactory to be now able to state that this event has come to pass, and that M. de Reutern has been enabled this year to show a balance on the right side of his budget.

It is a proof, and a solid one, of the improvements that can take place in Russia, and a standing monument of the ability and patriotic devotedness of the Minister of Finance, who may be justly proud that his eight years' labour has culminated in placing his country in a state of financial prosperity never reached before.

The value of Government securities has materially increased, and native Russians are now large investors in their own stocks: five per cent. bonds, which were issued by the Crown as payment to the nobles for their serfs, and which were, in 1866, sold as low as sixty-eight, are now quoted eighty-eight. Money is comparatively plentiful, the hoards of the peasants are brought to light; and the rouble, which was in 1866 only worth twenty-six pence, now obtains thirty-three pence. Russian paper-money may therefore be said to have risen in value twenty-five per cent. in five years.

The returns of fire insurance and life assurance show a considerable and steady increase,—one of the surest signs of the progress in intelligence of the people.

A liberally-inclined Government uses its best endeavour to encourage and defend trade and manufactures ; while the latter branch of industry, not yet fifty years old, has already reached very respectable proportions.

The resources of the Russian Empire are vast : whether we take her eighty millions of people, her mineral riches, her millions of acres of corn-growing country, her vast steppes of pasture land, her wealth in timber, her yet undeveloped coal-fields, her fisheries, or her geographical position as master of the East, the germ is seen of that great importance to which this great Muscovite Empire is slowly but yet surely rising.

What will be the destiny of that mighty state few can tell. The power which the sovereigns of Russia will hold in their hands will exceed anything experienced by the present generation.

Let us, in conclusion, express a hope that the life of His Imperial Majesty may be spared for many years to come, that he may be enabled to add to the blessings which he has already given to his people, and that the future Czars of this imperial kingdom may take for their model

---

Alexander Nikolaievitch, and devote, as he has done, their time, their endeavours, and their ability to the welfare of their subjects and the consolidation of their empire.

BOTACHEFF.

WYMAN AND SONS, PRINTERS, GREAT QUEEN STREET, LONDON, W.C.

PRESS CRITICISMS ON " RUSSIA IN 1870 "—*continued*.

" A very interesting and amusing book, full of information, not in a cumbrous mass, but neatly packed, each fact with an appropriate anecdote ready to be carried off by the memory."—*Globe*.

" The author is an acute and intelligent observer, and his long residence in the country, and familiar intercourse with the people, give to his statements a weight which is so often lacking in the tales of travellers. We most cordially recommend the book; it will be found as instructive as it is readable."—*Echo*.

" Mr. Barry has written a book really full of valuable information in a quiet and sensible manner."—*Literary World*.

" A very readable and pleasant book about Russia, and one which is the result of personal knowledge. The reader feels that Russia has been made to live before him in its social aspects."—*The Field*.

" Mr. Herbert Barry has special qualifications for the task he has undertaken; he has lived on intimate terms with all classes of the people, and writes in a style which enlists the reader's belief in his good faith. His book is well worthy of being read; it abounds with facts."—*Daily News*.

" Mr. Barry writes from an eminently practical stand-point, speaks of things of which he has an intimate acquaintance, and tells of people among whom he has lived and moved. He gives little, if any, hearsay evidence, and has a strong objection to writers who do so."—*Home News*.

" The book of Mr. Barry is chiefly a record of what he saw, and of the conclusions he came to. He was for the greater part of the time deep in the country, away from foreigners, and in close intercourse with natives, large numbers of whom he had under his immediate supervision. In addition, he resided some time in Moscow, and travelled very extensively in Russia and Siberia. We can cordially recommend it as the best book on that country (Russia) that has been published within the last ten years, and hope that it may find many readers."—*The Nation* (New York).

" This is a very interesting work concerning the Russia of the present day, a country with which the author, as a long resident there, is thoroughly acquainted."—*Weekly Paper*.

" There is much in the volume under consideration deserving of careful perusal; those who are desirous of comparing the social and political institutions of *old* and *new* Russia will find an ample store of fact in ' Russia in 1870.' We cordially recommend it."—*The Traveller*.

" That the writer of the present volume is a man in whom we may put implicit confidence can hardly be doubted; it is the record of the matured experiences of the resident as opposed to the mere impressions and second-hand stories of the tourist. We must reluctantly close our notice of a book which for valuable information and sustained interest is second to none."—*Standard*.

LONDON:

WYMAN & SONS, 74-75, GREAT QUEEN STREET;

AND OF ALL BOOKSELLERS.

THE PUBLISHING COMPANY,

LIMITED,

7, QUALITY COURT, CHANCERY LANE,

LONDON, W.C.

THE PUBLISHING COMPANY, LIMITED, publish approved Works at their own Cost, or on Commission, according to arrangement. Authors and possessors of Manuscripts requiring Terms, Estimates, or other Particulars, should apply to the Manager.

THE PUBLISHING COMPANY,

LIMITED,

7, QUALITY COURT, CHANCERY LANE,

LONDON, W.C.